THE PUNISHMENT ROOM

THE PUNISHMENT ROOM

Zara Devereuz

LIBRIS

X LIBRIS

First published in Great Britain in 2003 by X Libris
This paperback edition published in 2011 by X Libris

Copyright © 2003 by Zara Devereux

The moral right of the author has been asserted.

A CIP catalogue record for this book
is available from the British Library.

ISBN 978-0-7499-5486-4

Printed and bound in Great Britain by
Clays Ltd, St Ives plc

Papers used by X Libris are natural, renewable and
recyclable products sourced from well-managed forests and certified
in accordance with the rules of the Forest Stewardship Council.

Mixed Sources
Product group from well-managed
forests and other controlled sources
www.fsc.org Cert no. SGS-COC-004081
© 1996 Forest Stewardship Council

X Libris
An imprint of
Little, Brown Book Group
100 Victoria Embankment
London EC4Y 0DY

An Hachette UK Company
www.hachette.co.uk

www.littlebrown.co.uk

CHAPTER

1

Caitlin was tempted to switch on the telly to drown out the excited voices on the stairs and issuing from the bedsits that had turned the once gracious Armstrong Lodge into a student abode. She could hear her fellow tenants even with her door tight shut. Not quite housesharers, for they each had their own bathroom and small but adequate kitchenette, yet close enough to make her aware of being the odd one out.

Everyone was in a spin, anticipating the end-of-year bash at Antonia's wine-bar, a favourite watering hole for graduates and lecturers alike – the younger, unmarried, like-to-think-themselves hip ones, that is. Most of the students were now qualified and off to conquer the world, apart from Caitlin who was undecided. The prospect of teaching classes of hulking, crop-headed lads and feisty girls with attitude scared her to death. Once she had dreamed of bringing the glory of the English language to the next generation. The reality of a teacher-training stint in a comprehensive school had put a stop to that.

'You've just got to come along to Antonia's,' her friend Saskia had said. 'It'll be a laugh,' then she had added slyly, 'Tom will be there. You fancy him, don't you, Caitlin? Well, this is your chance. Get into something sexy and go for it. Knock him dead. He's a big-headed bastard and has a dick to die for, but he's not all that great in bed. He rushes it, convinced that the girl is duty-bound to come when he does.'

'Oh? I'm not interested,' Caitlin had lied, wishing she could control the hot blood that rushed to her cheeks.

Tom Fitzgerald, the best-looking man at Granchester University. Many a time she had wistfully watched him swaggering across the quad, his hands thrust deep in the pockets of his baggy chinos or, secretly admiring, stood among the spectators while he, resplendent in cricket whites, had proved himself ace bowler of the St Alban's College team. And he had become her masturbation fantasy, eclipsing the movie actors who had once helped her to orgasm.

'I think you're telling porkies,' Saskia had teased. 'Oh, come on. You don't get out enough. All work and no play makes Caitlin a very dull girl,' and she had given her an affectionate squeeze, drowning her in warm waves of exotic perfume and the personal scent of her hair and body.

Standing alone in her shabby room, Caitlin regretted capitulating to the forthright Saskia. Her surroundings added to her depression, the threadbare upholstery of the settee-cum-bed, the tatty floor-covering, peeling paintwork, battered utensils and chipped china betraying a long line of inhabitants before her, all similar, all aspiring – or not, as the case might be. How could she possibly invite Tom back here even if, by a miracle, he agreed to come?

She knew she had been lucky to get this accommodation when she arrived in Granchester three years ago, but now she couldn't wait to shake the dust from her feet. The finals were over and soon she would don a gown and mortar board and go up to accept her scroll from the Dean. She wondered if her mother or father would turn up to witness her moment of glory, but doubted it. Their divorce had not been amicable, and now he was in America and she was in Japan.

'I've nothing to wear,' she moaned aloud. 'And whatever I put on, Tom won't notice me. Saskia is stunning and doesn't care how much she shows, and all the other girls will be flashing sequinned tops and skimpy skirts. They're so confident. Why can't I feel like that?'

The mirror above the chest of drawers threw back her reflection: softly contoured face, big green eyes often concealed by reading glasses, a wide ox-bow mouth, and hair that had a strawberry blond tinge crying to be brought out. She had never managed to get up the nerve even to try a colour rinse.

She rooted through the wardrobe, pulling out and discarding one item after another – tops, skirts, boots and shoes. There was nothing there remotely suitable for tonight. Much of her stuff came from charity shops; most students were notoriously poor – not Saskia, of course – and Caitlin had bought each item for its serviceable quality. Except for one. There at the back, decently shrouded in a clear plastic dry-cleaning bag, hung her disastrous mistake. She had been contemplating taking it back, this silly impulse purchase which had lured her by its colour, brevity and designer label. There had been a fancy-dress party in the offing and she had kidded herself she'd wear it then. She never had, losing her nerve at the last moment and opting for something less eye-catching. But now she wondered: dare she put it on? Why the hell not? They were all going their separate ways very soon. It wouldn't matter if she made a fool of herself, just this once. And, who knows, it might make Tom sit up and take notice.

She lifted down the dress and freed it from hanger and covering. Once again she thrilled at the sight of it. Slimline and slinky, made of moss-green silk woven with sparkling threads, the bodice, which perfectly cradled her breasts, was low-necked, sleeveless and had narrow rhinestone straps. The skirt fitted her hips and then fell into handkerchief points below her calves. She remembered paying ten pounds for it and had regretted her extravagance ever since – until now. She spread it out on the bed, gloating over it. She had already showered, worked body lotion into her skin and given her nails another coat of lacquer. She usually opted for pale pink because it went with anything. Now, almost defiantly, she had taken up a bottle of frosted green and applied it on top.

Seems like I've already decided to give the dress a whirl, she thought and a frisson of excitement crawled down her spine. Why not go the whole hog and try out that underwear I couldn't resist the other day? It had been reduced in a sale, so Caitlin hadn't felt too bad about buying it, though

4

she had no idea when she might wear it. Now could be the moment. That's the trouble with me, she thought, while taking the set of black lace panties, brassière and suspender belt from their wrapping, I'm always having fantasies in which I either appear in public wearing nothing but these, or in private with someone like Tom, but I'm too scared to ever make them come true.

Of course, she had tried on the lingerie when she came back from purchasing it, and had been so excited by the view of herself looking positively tarty, that she had fallen back on the bed, still attired like a whore, and rubbed herself to completion, an act that made her burn with shame but which sometimes got out of control.

Thinking of this made her ache with longing, and fresh juice seeped from her vulva. She could feel her labial wings swelling and her ardent clitoris poking from its hood. Her hands were clumsy with haste as she settled her firm breasts in the bra cups, fingers flicking over the rosy-brown nipples, making them crimp. She then fastened the hooks at the back, clipped the belt round her waist and pulled down the suspenders. She fetched a pair of fishnet stockings from a drawer, sat on the bed and carefully rolled them so that she might put her feet in these seductive garments without ruining them. She worked them up her legs, slowly and sensually and could not resist moving her thumbs across her bare belly, feathering through her sparse fair bush and giving her clitoris a few well-aimed strokes. She gasped, thrust her pubis forward and up, then exerted control and concentrated on clipping the suspenders to the lacy welts. Finally she stood and twisted round so that she could view herself in the mirror, checking to make sure the seams were straight.

Nothing else about her had changed, but this naughty underwear made her feel wicked and wanton and she rummaged under the bed for a pair of plain black court shoes. When she put them on the illusion was complete. The heels bunched her calves and thighs and added inches to her height. She stood tall, spine straight, tits raised to heaven, and struck a pose like a pole-dance diva, arrogant, insolent, challenging. Ah, if I could only look at Tom this way, she sighed, tumbling down from this sexy high.

Do it, advised her alto ego. Come on to him. Make him want to eat pussy. Say to him, 'Good boy, that's it, good doggie, gobble me up!'

My God! Where did I learn to talk so dirty? she asked herself, shocked. Is this the real me, hidden away inside? A wild thing behind that prissy, goody-goody exterior.

Now footsteps and laughter passed her door, the other inmates clattering down the stairs, through the hallway and out. She expected Saskia's peremptory knock at any moment and pulled on her panties, then hurried over her make-up, a tad heavier than usual. Her hair posed a problem, long and thick and straight, so she swept the sides back off her face and fastened them with jewelled combs. This accentuated her eyes and cheekbones and she was halfway satisfied with the result.

And there was Saskia, shouting, 'Are you ready? The taxi's waiting.'

'Coming,' Caitlin replied, picked up her bag, shrugged a pashmina over her shoulders and made sure all the lights were out before leaving the room and locking the door.

6

Antonia, proprietress of the wine bar, was a stat-
uesque Italian, black-haired, dark-eyed, vivacious
and supremely confident. She talked a lot, each
word accompanied by an expressive gesture. Her
husband, Carlo, was short, stout and balding, but
attractive in his own way. He and Antonia argued
non-stop, but without animosity. They just liked
the sound of their own voices. Saskia had spent
many hours in the bar, not only drinking or on the
pull, but philosophising with the amiable couple.
She had picked up a smattering of Italian, but
usually they spoke English, apart from dramatic
statements that sounded so much more emphatic
in their own tongue.

As usual, Saskia arrived a little late that night,
putting into practice one of the few tips her irre-
sponsible mother had given her, that of making
an appearance after everyone else. It was like a
punctuation mark. She was pleased that Caitlin
had followed her advice and made an effort: she
wasn't at all bad looking when she tried.

They had both been at the university for eighteen
months before becoming acquainted. A vacancy at
Armstrong Lodge had brought them together
when Saskia had moved in. But even then, they
hadn't become bosom-buddies. Caitlin was so
reserved, and most of the time she looked anxious
and lonely. Sometimes when passing Caitlin's door
and wondering whether to knock, Saskia would
hear the strains of classical music coming through
it and this would stop her. If Caitlin was a culture
vulture, then they would have little in common.
But she had made the effort to be friendly and,
gradually, a little of Caitlin's ice had melted. Saskia
was very pleased to see that Caitlin was wearing a

daring dress and more war paint than usual.

'You look yummy,' she said as they elbowed their way to the bar. 'What are you drinking?'

'Thanks. I'll have orange juice, please,' Caitlin said nervously, wrapping her pashmina round her like a washerwoman's shawl.

'You won't,' Sakia replied with asperity. 'You'll have wine, like me, and for fuck's sake, take off that poncho thing. It ruins your image.'

Saskia was dressed in retro hippy gear. A floaty tangerine skirt, a pink strapless cotton top with no bra, elasticated at waist and chest, and so thin that her nipples stood out proud, a macramé belt slung low on her hips, and wedge-heeled thong sandals. Her hair was mussed and ringletted and flowing like a dusky cloud over her shoulders and halfway down her back. Her use of eyeliner and mascara was theatrical – so was the scarlet slash of her mouth. She had taken an arts course, intending to become an interior designer, though had been far-sighted enough to study computers, too. The idea of the bohemian lifestyle appealed enormously. She was liberal minded and a free spirit. Bi-sexual, she enjoyed the best of both worlds – open-handed, open-hearted, but shrewd and streetwise. In many ways, Caitlin could not have had a better teacher.

It was eight-thirty and the place was already crowded. 'Let's see if we can find a table,' Saskia suggested and, holding their glasses, they eased through the crowd. Dance music throbbed from overhead speakers, but there was hardly room to breathe, let alone dance. She scanned the room as best she could, remarking to Caitlin above the din, 'There's no sign of Tom, but then it's still early.'

Someone touched her backside, a finger that

lingered, finding her bottom crack through the flimsy cotton. She swing round, almost spilling her drink, and exclaimed, 'Oh, shit, it's you, Jerry. What the hell do you want?'

'Don't be like that,' he said with an oily grin. He was a stocky, unprepossessing individual with thinning ginger hair who had pursued her with dogged determination from the word go. His father had made his money through steel, and Jerry Robinson had bought his way into the university scene, unpopular but usually good for a handout. Hungry students weren't proud, but Saskia had a generous father who gave her an allowance and regularly cleared her overdrafts, so she could afford to be nasty to Jerry and had no intention of accepting his cock inside her.

'Piss off, Jerry,' she now said clearly, but he was determined and she was wedged in anyway. She felt his hot hand groping under her skirt, and the sweaty palm landing on her rear, his fingers edging round the string of her tanga.

'I know you're wet,' he said, leering at her, his face on a level with hers. 'You're a horny bitch, Saskia.'

Saskia toyed with the idea of chucking her drink in his face and wasting good red plonk. But rescue was at hand.

'Is this jerk annoying you?' asked the tall, rangy young man who materialised at her elbow. Not Tom, though he wasn't far behind, but Tom's friend, Hugh O'Mara, an American undergraduate on an exchange scheme. His deep Southern drawl went straight to her loins, just as if he had penetrated her physically. Saskia had clocked him earlier in the term, but hadn't been able to manipulate a meeting, and then the pressure of exams had taken over.

'It's fuck all to do with you,' Jerry growled, his face puce.

'D'you want him to stop?' Hugh asked, his brown eyes regarding her with a look that made her clitoris throb.

'Tell him to get his finger out of my pants.'

'You heard the lady. You're not welcome, pal,' Hugh said, looming over Jerry. With a shrug, Jerry withdrew, annoyance and frustration flashing in his little piggy eyes.

Saskia knew that he wasn't a man to take rebuffs kindly, and that he had too much influence in the college to risk offending, but now she didn't care. Her time there was over and the future shone brightly. She was moving to London to sign up with an established designer (a friend of her mother's) who was high in the popularity stakes in TV changing-room programmes and much in demand by stars wanting complete and startling alterations to their house.

Saskia knew she could do it. Chameleon-like, she had the ability to fit in almost anywhere. She was as familiar with streetspeak as any urban guerrilla or could adopt the drawling accent of a Sloane. Daddy was a landowner and into politics, and she had been born with the proverbial silver spoon. City houses in elegant areas, a stately home inherited by her upper-crust mother, boarding school, finishing school, and university. It had all been hers. Twats like Jerry didn't stand an earthly, but he persisted.

'You're looking great tonight. I love the blouse. It shows off your tits,' he said, greasily.

'Hi, Jerry. At it again, you sad git,' said Tom, grinning down at Saskia.

10

Jerry retired in the face of so much opposition, and Saskia settled down to the serious business of the evening – that of getting laid. The bar was even more crowded than earlier. She was crushed between Hugh and Tom and, despite her earlier unkind remarks about him to Caitlin, she was filled with the exhilarating feeling that she wanted to make love to as many personable men as possible that night.

Jerry had been right on one count; she was aware of the wetness between her thighs, dampening the narrow crotch of her pantics, a long, languorous spasm raising the sliver of flesh that was the seat of her sensation, while her enfolding labial wings thickened. As Hugh pressed closer to her, partly through circumstances but mostly due to design, his arm brushed against her nipples. They crimped. He glanced down and a smile hovered around his wide, generous mouth. She imagined how it would feel to have his lips slurping at her clit.

'How about it, Saskia? Are you up for it?' Tom murmured close to her ear. 'Hugh needs an introduction to the English girl's way of love. There's this distressing rumour among foreigners that our women are frigid. I've never found that. Have you? And I'm sure you'd know. I'll bet you're into eating pussy. Do you do it with your little friend here? The inestimable Caitlin.'

Saskia had almost forgotten about her and now reacted, conscious smitten. 'D'you think I'd tell you if I was? It would have nothing to do with you, Tom.'

'Oh, come on!' he mocked, and one of his big hands reached round and caressed her shoulder-blade. 'You'd let me watch, wouldn't you? Two

11

girls. One man who'd show 'em what they were missing.'

'You wish,' she mouthed, reaching the bar and attracting Antonia's attention.

'I'll buy this round,' Hugh offered. 'Same again?'

'Not for me,' put in Caitlin timidly. 'I've had one already.'

'Go on. Try another,' urged Tom, and Saskia wondered what he was up to. Did he really intend to screw Caitlin? Or was his mind running smutty scenarios in which she and Caitlin appeared naked and nubile and sucking each other's clits?

A glance at Caitlin's face assured her that this wasn't a good idea. She was wearing the mesmerised look of a rabbit confronted by a stoat. For all her brash talk earlier, Saskia was worried about Caitlin, and had an urge to shield her from a big bad world full of predatory men. She felt sisterly towards her, maybe even maternal. Tom would chew her up and spit her out when he had done. There was nothing for it. Saskia was compelled to save Caitlin from him. What a sacrifice, she thought cynically. She was up for it that night. Tom and Hugh and maybe one other. What about that thin-featured boy a little further down the bar. He couldn't keep his eyes off her.

'Tom. Who is that?' she asked, pointing.

For an answer, Tom shouted, 'Stan, old lad. Come and meet some friends of mine.'

Stan didn't need asking twice, a Northerner who, it turned out, was studying engineering. He was twenty, a fresher in his first year. Keen on sport, but keener still on meeting college totty and getting laid. He'll do, Saskia decided, running experienced eyes down his lean body in its khaki vest and combats. He was muscular from all that sport and sessions in the gym, and had dark hair gelled into spikes, blue eyes and a promising bulge in the fly area. Her cunt felt like it was a queen and needed more than one subject to bow down and worship it.

But, meanwhile, what was she going to do about Caitlin? She was practically a virgin, or so she maintained, speaking only of an unfortunate experience with an insensitive dork long before she came to uni. He had been a handsome lad whose kisses had excited her, her young, untried body tingling at his touch, her emotions aroused along with her hopes of a romantic, happy-ever-after idyll. The reality, when he had inexpertly pushed his cock into her, had put her off men She hadn't tried again.

So-oo, what now? Saskia thought. Maybe it's best to simply throw her in at the deep end. Sink or swim. I shall be there to do my lifeguard act. Then again, it might be better to leave well alone. After all, we'll be decamping very soon and it's quite likely we'll drift apart and maybe never meet again. Yet that makes me unhappy. Caitlin is sincere and honest, a rarity these days, and it would be nice to have someone like her to fall back on when things go pear-shaped, as they are bound to do sometimes. I'm not as tough as I make out. I'd appreciate a friend.

'What are we doing at kicking-out time?' Hugh asked, and in the midst of that maelstrom of chat and laughter and music, Saskia felt as if they were alone at the top of a mountain.

'Come back to mine,' she replied at once. 'We'll party on.'

Hers consisted of a large room under the eaves,

not so much lofty as quaint, with sloping ceilings and dormer windows at floor level. It had once housed servants, no doubt, when Armstrong Lodge had been a gentleman's residence in the best part of Granchester. The room wasn't simply spacious – it was enormous. She kept it warm in winter by feeding the radiators, having her own gas meter that also fired the power shower in the en suite bathroom and the cooker in the neat kitchen, though Saskia was a microwave dinner or eating out person. Cookery did not appeal. Whereas the other bedsits were sparsely furnished, Saskia's parents had made sure hers was tastefully, even luxuriously equipped.

I'll be quite sorry to leave it, she thought as she unlocked the door and walked in, waving to her friends to follow. 'Coffee, anyone?' she asked. 'The galley's over there.'

'I'll do it,' Caitlin volunteered, followed by Tom.

'What are friends for?' Saskia asked, plonking herself down in the middle of the six-foot wide bed. It stood against one wall, tented in gold silk draped from the rafters, gorgeously spread with a Turkish throw. It could certainly accommodate a threesome, even a foursome, and Saskia kicked off her shoes and curled her toes in the sumptuous quilt.

She eyed Hugh and Stan. The American came across and sat beside her, a can of lager in one hand. He set it down on the nightstand near an antique lamp. 'You got it good,' he remarked.

'I was lucky, but Daddy pulled a few strings,' she vouchsafed. 'He knew a man who knew a man, et cetera.'

'My digs aren't anything like this,' gloomed Stan. 'I'm sharing with mates.'

14

'And you're staying on,' Saskia said, her skirt riding up above her knees, giving them an uninterrupted view of her long, sunkissed legs.

It was late June and, so far, the weather had been warm. She had spent time near-naked on a lounger in the overgrown, jungly garden. It was secluded and wild, even though the street was just beyond the high stone wall. No one wanted to do an 'Alan Titchmarsh', so it did its own thing. Saskia knew that when she settled in London priority number one would be a garden, roof or otherwise. Papa Higgins was already negotiating a property for her.

'That's right. I'm getting a job through the summer. I've a hell of a student loan to pay back one day.' Stan pretended to be Jack-the-lad, but was awkward when it came to joining her and Hugh on the bed.

She wouldn't allow it anyway, until he had taken a taper to the candles on the mantelpiece, on the low table near the settee and in niches on the walls, which supplemented the bedside lamp. These gave the room a mysterious, mellow glow. Incense in oriental burners sent sweet-smelling smoke spiralling up, and a basket filled with multi-shaped and many-coloured condoms stood at the ready. The atmosphere was decidedly voluptuous, just as Saskia liked it. Oh, she could enjoy a shag up against a wall in an alley, or on the backseat of a car, but for preference, and to give the event a kind of significance, she revelled in the sensuality of her own bed.

Caitlin returned with a tray of coffee mugs. She was flushed, even animated, and wore a bemused expression whenever she glanced at Tom. Saskia wondered what he had been doing while they waited for the kettle to boil. Dipped a hand down to her fork, maybe, or feathered his fingers over her nipples?

Love is a sad and sorry business, she thought, and I never want to do it. Caitlin, on the other hand, seems to have this old-fashioned notion that to enjoy sex one has to be emotionally involved. It's quite sweet really and, I suppose, to be envied, yet how vulnerable it makes her. She patted the place beside her and said, 'Sit down, Caitlin. Relax. You're far too tense.'

Hugh was behind her, propping her up, his long legs stretched on either side of hers. By leaning back into his crotch she could feel the hard bar of his cock and wriggled against it. Tom was watching, sidling closer to Caitlin, and Stan leaned against the bedpost, a hand moving up and down over his fatigue-covered erection. Game, set and match, Saskia thought, and arched her neck so that Hugh could reach her mouth. His kiss was long, strong and perfect, and his bridgework divine. No off-putting halitosis there, just white, even, well-cared-for teeth and his breath was fresh, too, only slightly spiced with lager.

Saskia began to lose it. Hugh's cock felt hot and damp against her bottom and her position had worked the Lycra gusset up into the vertical line of her cleft. It was pressing tantalisingly on her swollen clit. She broke away from Hugh's kiss and gazed at Stan through slitted lids and saw the very large bulge inside his combats and the way in which his hand was kneading it.

'Get it out for me, Stan,' she whispered huskily. 'In fact, all you boys flop 'em out. Let's see who has the biggest.'

'You mean it? Yes ... sure ... OK,' Stan mumbled, and she guessed that this was the first time he had been asked to show it.

She nodded and the thought of his fat shaft made her shiver. Her curiosity knew no bounds when it came to comparing the length, girth and all-over splendour of the male appendage. Hugh freed himself from her and stood by the bed, taking off his shirt, then his trainers, his jeans and boxer shorts. Meanwhile Stan had kicked off his boots and socks, dropped his trousers and, naked apart from his vest, stood there displaying his wares. Saskia goggled. She'd seen some cocks in her time but his took the biscuit. He continued to fondle it and she had serious doubts as to whether she could take it inside her. It was huge, a massive stem with a mushroom-shaped head already glistening with pre-come.

She beckoned and Stan came closer. She sat up and opened her legs so that he was between them, then she took that enormous helm between her lips. Stan groaned and pressed closer. She backed off a little, for it was already ramming into her throat. Poor boy! To be blessed or cursed with such a monster! Yet it was a thing to be proud of, even with the inconvenience of housing it, coping with it, finding a fanny willing and able to accommodate it. She buried her face in his thick, wiry bush, inhaling the strong odour of randy male, groping between his legs and weighing his testicles, a pair of plump fruit which matched his dick in size. She wondered briefly how he managed this equipment when taking part in sporting events.

She drew back and breathed deeply. His quivering prick stood out like a broomhandle, wet with her saliva and his jism. She shot a sidelong glance at Caitlin. She was sitting there stunned, her face crimson, unable to tear her eyes away from Stan's monster. Then Hugh presented his in all its naked glory – short, very thick and naked of foreskin, the helm bare and red and pierced with a small gold bar through the upper and lower edge of the corona. This was a wonderful bonus for Saskia, but Caitlin looked as if she were about to rise and run for it.

'Wait,' Saskia said to her, and pulled her blouse off over her head. 'You'll enjoy this. Start by watching us, then you may find you want to join in.'

'Yes, come on, Caitlin,' urged Tom, already stripped to the waist and hopping about on one foot as he took off his loafers. 'I want to see you naked. I know that you're inexperienced. Let me show you how wonderful it can be.'

Saskia squirmed her hips out of her skirt and then whipped off the tiny G-string. Now she was bare, her breasts soaring upwards, her nipples hard as cob-nuts, her slim waist, flat belly and thighs golden brown, with a perfect seamless tan. Her mound was covered by springy black floss with an even darker strip running down the middle to disappear into her delta. Now Stan was bending over her, touching her teats and she moaned with pleasure, while Hugh lay beside her, reached across and parted her legs, fingering her wet snatch. She pushed hard against his hand, rubbing her clit up and down on his middle digit, ready, oh so ready to come.

Tom, completely nude and sporting a fine erection, smiled at Caitlin. 'Shall I help you to undress?'

Caitlin shot to her feet, hands clasped against

her breasts as if he had suggested molesting her. 'No,' she shouted. 'I don't want to do it this way. I thought . . . hoped . . . we might take it slowly, get to know one another . . .'

'And what better way than this?' he answered smoothly, his hand skimming down her bare arm.

'I don't think so. Goodnight, Tom.'

Saskia saw her make for the door as if the hounds of hell were after her.

'Strange girl,' Tom drawled, and lowered his agile body to rest on Saskia's other side.

Just for a moment, she worried about her timid friend, then forgot almost immediately as Hugh rolled on a condom, positioned himself between her legs and edged his shiny dome into her very wet entrance, while Tom eased a finger into her cleft and manipulated her throbbing clit. Stan knelt so that she could take his dick into her mouth again and she used her free hand to palpate Tom's long and meaty cock. She was whirled high on a rollercoaster of pleasure, her first orgasm exploding in a shower of stars. Then it was like a game of musical chairs as the men changed places and, at one point, she was thoroughly plugged by Stan's almost-too-big-for-comfort tool. The bed became a vehicle for pleasure, like a raft floating in some tropical, exotic sea, and Saskia was satisfied – or very nearly – coming again and again, while her three lovers struggled to keep up with her.

She slept at last, sprawled among the pillows, cradled in arms and with legs wrapped around her. As the next day dawned, her lovers were reviving, ready to service her again.

CHAPTER

2

T he letter lay among the heap of mail on the hallstand. Typed and official looking, it was addressed to Miss Caitlin Colbert.

After a wretched night during which she had tossed and turned, listened to Saskia having hectic sex overhead, reviewed her life and found it wanting, Caitlin had got up early, shrugged on her uninspiring towelling robe and trailed barefoot down the stairs. At least the letter brought a spark of interest, lightening her despondency, and she carried it back to her room, dropped a teabag in her Winnie the Pooh mug and took them both to bed. I mustn't drink ever again, she thought, head thumping. Red wine! All right for those that are used to it. Not me.

But the hangover wasn't the cause of her black mood. It was Tom. When they had made coffee in Saskia's kitchen he had seemed so keen, hinting that they might go to a play together – a touring company was visiting the Students' Union and performing an Ayckbourn comedy. She had momentarily dreamed of a meeting of souls, someone with whom she could share intellectual pursuits, and thought that Saskia must have been wrong about him. Yes, he had touched her up, but gently, and she had liked it. She had looked into his grey eyes and imagined that he shared her dreams. Then the wine had given her a false sense of optimism. Why shouldn't someone like him fall for her? She had much to offer a man – companionship and love as well as sex – and, in that heady moment before the kettle clicked off, she had wanted him with a desperation that went way beyond endurance. She had been prepared to sleep with him that night, but the scene in and around Saskia had brought her to her senses.

She had come down to earth with a bump, realising that all Tom wanted was to get into her knickers and add another name to his list of conquests. Disgusted with him and all of them, including Saskia, she had retreated to her room, sad and disillusioned once again.

Now it promised to be a fine day. There were things to do, a thesis to print out and hand in, the outfitters to visit where she would hire her graduation gown. None of these appealed. She just wanted to hide away. She couldn't face Saskia, sure that she and her lovers, including the perfidious Tom, had made fun of her when she'd gone. She felt unable to trust anyone ever again. The house was unnaturally quiet. No one was stirring. Then she remembered that it was Saturday. The best part of the university crowd would be nursing aching heads and regrets and ruing the money wasted on booze and waking up in bed with the wrong people.

I'm glad it's not me, she thought, and meant it.

The tea started to clear away her cobwebs and she ripped open the envelope. Yes, a very official letter, but not from the bank, or the uni, or even the teacher-training course which was one of her options.

It was headed Wardour, Price and Griffen, Solicitors, and the address was College Street, Granchester, and it read: Dear Miss Colbert, If you care to call on us at your earliest convenience, you will receive notification of the last will and testament of the recently deceased Miss Mary Macey. Please phone for an appointment, Yours, W.A. Griffen.

Caitlin reached for her glasses and scanned it again. Mary Macey, her great-aunt. She remembered her now, and little vignettes flashed across her brain from holidays spent in Cornwall when she was a child, of Father and Mother, quarrelling even then, and of a house overlooking a bay. Not simply a house, more of a hotel. And a woman, tall, handsome, unmarried, ruling the establishment – her mother had called her Aunt Mary. So what had this to do with herself? She hadn't visited there or kept up correspondence for years, apart from the obligatory Christmas card, and neither had her mother, as far as she knew. There seemed to have been a breakdown in communication around the time of the divorce.

Could it be that Mary Macey had remembered her and made some small bequest? Anything would be welcome to go towards settling her bank loan. I'll ring now, she thought. Then, oh damn, it's Saturday. I'll give it a whirl anyway. There may be someone there.

She just about managed to afford a mobile and checked on the time. It was after nine and any respectable office should be open. She let it ring, impatient to find out what this was all about. A woman replied at last, informing her that they closed at noon. Caitlin made an appointment, washed, dressed herself in a plain, no-nonsense skirt and jumper, removed last night's green nail polish, and arrived at the solicitor at eleven o'clock precisely.

It was a Regency house built by a cotton baron two centuries before, one in a terrace of identical buildings, with a basement, attics and steps leading up to the front door. Caitlin pressed the buzzer and a disembodied voice answered her. She gave her name and the door swung open. The hall had a black and white tiled floor, like a chess-board, a curving, delicate staircase that floated aloft – stone treads supported on fancy ironwork – and a marble statue of Adonis in a niche, his private parts discreetly covered by a fig leaf. A door to the right opened and a man came out.

'Ah, you must be Miss Colbert,' he said, and advanced to shake her by the hand. 'Come in, come in. I'm William Griffen, senior partner.'

He was dapper, sprightly and middle aged. He had kindly, twinkling eyes set in a ruddy face, and silvery hair brushed back from a high forehead. The photographs adorning the walls depicted him standing on the deck of a sailing ship, dressed in a navy blazer and yachting cap. Obviously a sporting man in his free time.

Cailtin, who had been acutely nervous, lost some of her shyness, feeling at ease with him and heartened by his avuncular manner. She took a chair opposite his with a wide, leather topped desk stretching between them. This, like every other piece of furniture, was in keeping with the house, apart from a state-of-the-art computer and fax machine.

'Well, now,' he began, shuffling papers, then looking up and peering at her. 'I expect you're wondering what this is about.'

'I am,' she confessed, sitting upright with her knees together and her hands clenched round the bag on her lap. 'I remember Miss Macey, just about . . . but it was a long time ago.'

'Of course, of course. She said as much in the letter she left with her solicitors who contacted me.'

'How did she know I was at Granchester University?'

'She had a card from you last Christmas, apparently, and guessed you would still be here. She was ill then, and died in April. It takes time for these matters to be sorted,' he explained.

'But why me? Why not my mother? Did she leave her something, too?' Caitlin asked, confused.

'Apparently she is not to benefit, apart from one painting which has some value. Only yourself. I think Miss Macey's letter will be self-explanatory,' and he handed it over.

Caitlin fished out her spectacles and perched them on her nose. The first thing she saw was the heading. It was in large, bold, sloping print: High Tides, Queensbury, North Cornwall. Five Star Hotel and Restaurant.

She pictured the place in her mind's eye. Time

rolled back and she could hear the seagulls crying as they wheeled and dipped overhead, and smell that salty, oceanic odour borne on the breeze from the wild waters outside the bay.

She read on. The letter had been written on a computer and this was a print out. Mary Macey had moved with the times, it seemed. It was addressed to Trewiddle and Penwarden, her legal eagles in Newquay. At first Caitlin's bewildered brain couldn't take it in, but a second reading clarified the situation and brought her up with a jolt.

Apart from the bequests made to the afore-mentioned friends and members of staff, the bulk of my assets, including stocks, shares and High Tides, shall pass to my great-niece, Caitlin Colbert, at present studying at Granchester University. When her parents divorced, against my wishes and advice, I determined that their unfortunate daughter should be my beneficiary. No child should be forced to witness the distressing break up of her parents' marriage. It must have affected her deeply. Her mother, Deborah Colbert, now Macdonald, is my next of kin, but she chose to make a life for herself elsewhere. Therefore, I wish Caitlin to inherit everything. I hope she will not squander this, but keep High Tides and continue to run it along the lines that have given it such a solid reputation.

Stunned, Caitlin lowered the letter, but kept her eyes fixed on it. 'I don't believe it,' she whispered at last. 'I never knew ... didn't expect anything like this.'

'It has no doubt come as a shock, but a not unpleasant one, I trust,' Griffen replied with a smile. 'It's not every day that I am called upon to impart such good news. You are rich, Miss Colbert. A woman of substance.'

'But I don't know what to do. I've never handled large sums of money before. It has always been a struggle to make ends meet.'

'I'm here to assist you,' he said. 'I can negotiate with Trewiddle and Penwarden and arrange the transfer of money and shares to your bank, who will in turn put you in touch with their financial advisers. Do you want to keep High Tides?'

'I don't know,' she answered, but the thought of selling it went against the grain.

'Why don't you take a trip to Queensbury and look around?' he suggested. 'You may find the idea of moving to the Cornish coast appeals to you. I know it would to me,' and he cast a fond eye at the picture of his boat. 'A grand place. One of my favourites. In fact, you might find I become a guest at your hotel. I could cruise round from Falmouth where the *Gadfly* is moored at the moment. I expect there's a marina close at hand.'

He's jumping the gun, isn't he? she thought, a multitude of scenarios rushing through her head. She didn't want to become a teacher, but what about a hotelier? The idea was terrifying. So much responsibility, and yet – and *yet* – she would be her own boss, no longer a dogsbody, but someone important, like Mary Macey. Fate had laid this gift in her lap. It would be churlish to toss it aside without at least giving it a look.

'When shall I be able to use some of the money?' she asked.

'It can be transferred as soon as you sign these papers and they are returned to Messrs Trewiddle and Co. But I strongly advise that you consult with a financier before you make any move,' he added anxiously, as if visualising her blowing the lot.

'I will. But I'd like to go down to Queensbury and view my property,' she said, though the use of the words did not come easily to her tongue. *My property!* When I've never owned a damn thing in my life, and was anticipating years of struggle ahead trying to clear my debts. And now, like a bolt out of the blue, I'm sole owner of a hotel that must be worth a cool two million, at least. Of course I want to go and see it. Now. At once!

'Inform my bank,' she said, almost imperiously. It was wonderful how much difference cash made. 'If they'll advance me a loan to take that trip to Cornwall, I'll go at once.'

Without hesitation, she signed the documents. Griffen rose when she did, accompanying her to the door. 'Don't worry, Miss Colbert,' he said. 'I'll do everything that is necessary. Arrange to see your bank manager next week. By that time he'll be au fait with the situation.'

The trilling of the phone penetrated Belle Godwin's dreams. She sighed, and tried to ignore it, but to her phones always needed answering. She could never resist finding out who was calling, even at seven-thirty in the morning when she was snuggled up in her wide bed in the arms of the nubile young waiter she had seduced last night.

The room was dappled with the bright, sunshiny light of a cloudless day that filtered through the chintz curtains. From below came the sounds of a

27

busy establishment stirring into life – footsteps, voices, the hum of a vacuum cleaner and the smell of coffee and full English breakfasts being prepared in the kitchen. Belle half sat, disengaging herself from Barry's grasp, though he muttered and protested and tried to wedge his hard-on in the crack of her bottom.

'Don't hang up,' she instructed the invisible caller, lifted the receiver from its cradle and said, with that on-the-ball efficiency she could turn on like a tap, 'Hello, this is High Tides. How may I help you?'

'Oh, yes, well, sorry to ring so early, but I'm intending to come down today,' said a breathless young voice from the other end. 'I'm Caitlin Colbert. Could I speak to Mrs Godwin?'

'This is she,' Belle replied, sitting upright now, pulling the quilt over her full breasts, and feathering her fingers through her tawny blond hair. Barry took the opportunity to press closer, obsessed by his morning erection and concerned only about putting it somewhere.

But Belle, now fully awake, was concentrating on what the caller was saying.

'I'm so pleased to be talking with you, Mrs Godwin. I expect Miss Macey's lawyers have told you about me.'

'That's right,' said Belle slowly, curious about, and somehow wary of, this great-niece who Mary Macey had made her heir. 'Naturally you want to come down and take a look around. I'll help you all I can. Miss Macey left me in charge. I'm the manageress, housekeeper, chief cook and bottle-washer. I've worked here for ten years.'

'So I understand,' the young woman answered,

and she sounded nervous and no threat at all, though Belle still wondered where she would stand now that High Tides was under new ownership.

Mary, a friend as well as her boss, had left her well provided for. She had more than enough to buy a cottage in the West Country, or a villa in Spain for that matter, but Belle was a creature of habit; she enjoyed her position at High Tides, was well known and liked in Queensbury and the surrounding district, and had no desire to up sticks. Recently divorced and still raw when she had applied for the job as Mary's second-in-command, she had soon settled into her role.

She was a social animal, possessed of wry good humour and the cynical way of looking at things that was necessary in the hotel and catering business. She had everything she wanted, including the pick of the men who came to work at the hotel – in the bars, the restaurant, kitchens or even as gardeners. Belle chose the staff herself, for their ability, but also for their looks, female as well as male. She liked brawn in men more than brains, broad shoulders, narrow hips and a promising package.

'When may we expect you, Miss Colbert?' she asked, easing down and parting her legs to give Barry access to her cunt. He gripped hold of one ample breast and bore it to his mouth, suckling like a baby.

'The train gets in to Newquay at six-twenty, all being well and the connections arriving on time.'

'I'll send a car for you. I look forward to meeting you,' and Belle ended the conversation with her usual calm which always reassured punters and staff alike. But it wasn't easy to keep her cool with Barry exploring between her thighs, then worming his way into her, finger buried to the knuckle.

'Well, well,' she commented, coiling herself round him, impatiently shifting his lips to her other breast while keeping her fingers rolling the wet, pointed tip of the teat he had been nibbling.

'Good news or bad?' he asked, looking up at her with a smile that she found far too cocky. He was getting above himself, just because she had chosen him to share her bed last night. He must realise that this didn't make him special, or that she necessarily planned a repeat performance.

'Probably good,' she replied cagily. The less he or any other member of staff knew about the changeover the better. 'We'll have to wait and see.'

'Meanwhile, we don't have to get up yet, do we? I've got this great big monster waiting to fuck you.'

'Mr Ramsey can cope with breakfasts, but he'll skewer your balls on a kebab stick if he thinks you're malingering. I'll have to be down in reception at nine; Friday is always busy, as you'll find out. Guests departing and new ones coming in, to say nothing of the extra weekend work in the restaurant,' she said, but had to admit to herself that Barry had a cheeky appeal – that's why she had selected him as her latest toyboy.

She might as well enjoy this while she could. It looked like she was soon going to be fully occupied with Caitlin, and she wanted to make a thorough job of showing her round and explaining the ramifications of running High Tides, though this would merely scratch the surface as it took years to really understand what was involved. She hadn't quite made up her mind, but thought her position would be more secure if Mary Macey's young relation decided to take over, instead of the place being bought out by a chain. Then indeed, Belle might be given her marching orders, ousted by managers experienced in the ways of group hotels.

'Let me go and have a pee first,' she said, swinging her legs over the edge of the mattress and then padding, naked, into the en suite bathroom.

She liked to be fresh for her lovers, and washed her pussy, then switched on her electric toothbrush to freshen her mouth. A quick application of roll-on deodorant, and she was ready for Barry. Never fully able to switch off even in the heat and rut of the bed, she tried to shove Caitlin Colbert to the back of her mind.

'Come on then, tiger,' she growled, sashaying towards him.

He reached out and pulled her down; he was tough and rather rough and she loved it, falling across him as he sprawled on his back. Belle sat astride him, knees clamped either side of his muscular torso. He was no thin, pasty wimp – he worked out, got the sun when he could and had sessions in the solarium at the gym. She reached down and rubbed her palm over his cock, feeling it surge. When she let go it slapped back against her buttocks.

He stuck out his tongue-tip and made little suggestive, wagging movements. She bent over and, using her own tongue, fenced with it, then invaded his mouth, exchanging saliva, tasting all the virile youthfulness of him, feeding on his lips, his gums, the soft lining of his inner cheeks. He moaned and she felt his cock dancing as he humped thin air. She dipped her pelvis, bringing pressure to bear on her fur-fringed vaginal lips. She rubbed her clit against his hairy belly, leaving a silvery trail of juice.

She slid down till his cock popped out before her and grasped it, loving to make any man's appendage perform for her. She pulled the foreskin back to fully expose the shiny wet glans, then shrouded it in flesh again so that nothing showed but the slit, repeating this game several times. Barry groaned with pleasure. Her clit tingled.

It was immensely satisfying to have this eager youth at her mercy. It gave her an intoxicating sense of power almost as strong as when she stood in the restaurant on a busy evening, seeing the well-heeled guests, the glittering silver utensils, the cut-glass goblets and fine china and the immaculately dressed waiters and waitresses serving exquisite dishes prepared in the kitchens. Above all things, Belle liked to be in charge. Would Caitlin Colbert pose a threat?

Forcing herself to forget about Caitlin, she gripped Barry's prick harder, and guided it between her teeth, dipping into the slit and tasting the salty tear that lingered there. She licked him languorously, running her tongue up his stem as if she were enjoying an ice-cream cone, then she took the whole of him into her mouth, moving up and down, with hardly a pause between strokes.

'You're a bloody marvel,' Barry gasped, a hand on either side of her head, using her hair like a halter to hold her to him.

Teasingly, she withdrew until only the very end of his bulging helm touched her lips. She knew he was about to come, so pressed firmly on his cock root, delaying the moment. His excitement was echoed in her groin. She didn't want to wait much longer, and started to suck him in earnest, milking him, her mouth working on his pulsing shaft, feeling it swell, hearing his gasps. She sucked harder, her cheeks caving in, and his hips jerked, his cock convulsed and a fountain of come spurted into her throat. She swallowed the torrent, but it continued to flow, dribbling across her lips and down her chin and bedewing her hair.

She let his cock fall away from her mouth, then smeared the residue over her neck and breasts. She was superstitious about young men's spunk; to her it had a magical quality, an elixir promising rejuvenation and eternal beauty.

'Get that condom on. It's my turn,' she cried happily.

She straddled Barry's face, felt his lips sucking at her clit, his tongue circling the engorged button. She held him fast between her thighs and rode him mercilessly, chasing her orgasm. She yelled as she reached the top of the wave, then tumbled down in a cascade of sparks. Spasms shook her vagina, and she rolled over with Barry on top of her, opened her legs wide and impaled herself on his ever-ready weapon. She took it deep inside her, pumping at it furiously to drain the very last sensations from her cunt. Scissoring her legs round his waist, she screamed as he rammed into her, until they both came again.

This is a tedious journey, Caitlin thought, settling in the carriage after having waited an hour at Exeter station for the connection to Newquay. I'll really have to get myself a car.

She had passed her driving test when she was eighteen, but what with university and her mother departing to Japan with her second husband, there had been no money or any necessity for her to purchase even an old banger. Things will alter now, she thought, hugging the secret to her. She had discussed her change of circumstances with no one except Mr Griffen and Mr Hodge, her bank manager. Both gentlemen had been most respectful, and she, it seemed, had asked the right questions and impressed them with her sober acceptance of her fortune. Money had been forthcoming, but it had taken a few days, so the earliest she could plan a visit had been yesterday. Her conversation with Mrs Godwin that morning had been reassuring. She sounded a friendly person.

Caitlin had successfully avoided Saskia and had kept very much to herself. She had rung her mother in Tokyo, and the conversation had not been pleasant. The phone line had been so clear they might have been in the same room, but Caitlin had been glad that they weren't; Mother was not at all pleased.

'I know all about it,' she had said crisply. 'Had a letter from her solicitors. All she left me was that gloomy old painting of a stag at bay that used to hang in the lobby. She did it on purpose, knowing how much I disliked it. You've done all right, by the sound of it. Trust her to pull a stunt like that. She didn't approve of me, and hated it when I divorced your father. It's a wonder she didn't leave everything to an animal sanctuary. What are you going to do? Keep the hotel?'

'I haven't decided,' Cailtin had replied, feeling guilty. It was perfectly fair and what Aunt Mary had wanted, but she still couldn't shake off the feeling that her mother should have inherited, not her.

'You could sell it, and then the world would be

34

your oyster. Come and stay with Sydney and me. He could put you in touch with the textile trade. You might even invest in his business.' The eager edge to her voice had warned Caitlin not to get involved. She didn't much like Sydney Macdonald. He was too oily, too fly. A canny operator who saw no reason not to exploit overseas workers if he could profit by it.

'I'm going to Queensbury at the weekend,' Caitlin had said, thankful that her mother was too far away to interfere. 'Then I'll make up my mind.'

Now she stared out at the passing landscape. They had left the undulating hills and gentle valleys of Devon and entered the bleaker clime of Cornwall, that mythical realm of King Arthur and Tintagel. Once across the Tamar Bridge and one was almost in another country. No shelter there from the fairies and pixies and 'knockers', those odd little goblins who lived in the tin mines, tap-tapping away in the galleries underground. The old legends came back to Caitlin and she remembered Aunt Mary recounting them. She couldn't wait to get to High Tides, excitement swamped apprehension. It was the biggest thing she had ever done, and that included going to university. She had been lonely there, and hoped that this time she might make a few friends, even if she sold up in the end.

She sat on the edge of her seat, attracting the attention of the man opposite who was reading a newspaper. He glanced across at her and smiled. She blushed, for he was personable in a conventional way. He had neatly styled, wavy hair, and a pinstriped suit, a white shirt and dark tie. There was a briefcase on the seat beside him.

'Your first visit here?' he inquired politely, folding up his paper and laying it aside.

'No,' she answered hesitatingly. Hadn't she been taught not to talk to strange men?

'On holiday?' he persisted, while the train rattled along, gaining speed as it approached its destination.

'Not exactly. I have business in Queensbury,' she said, wishing he'd go back to reading. Really, he had no right to impose himself on her, yet he was rather good looking, and she felt him accidentally – or was it on purpose? – place his foot alongside hers under the narrow table.

She wore thong sandals, her toes bare, and they responded to the feel of soft leather and the knowing way in which he touched her. All she had to do was draw away and he would say, 'I'm sorry,' and pull his foot back. She didn't move.

The train sped on, the sky lightened and, in the distance, she caught a glimpse of the huge white cones, residue from the china clay pits, that dominated the skyline, with the sea beyond. It was faraway, its blue meeting that of the horizon, but it was possible to get an inkling of spume and spray and waves.

'You look as if you've not been to the coast for a while,' the man said, and he seemed so harmless and friendly, admiring even, that she lost some of her reserve.

'I haven't, not since I was a child. For the past three years I've been at Granchester University. I was going to be a teacher . . . but now . . .'

'You've changed your plans. Something to do with a boyfriend, perhaps?'

Oh, dear, why do men always assume that there

has to be sex in it somewhere? she wondered, beginning to understand why Saskia had such a low opinion of them.

'I haven't got a boyfriend.' She realised too late that this was unwise.

He leaned forward, smiling roguishly and saying, 'I don't believe it. Not a pretty girl like you. What's wrong with all the chaps at Granchester? Have they decided to board the wrong bus?'

He's so cheesy, she concluded, and the chill in her voice could have melted permafrost. 'I haven't met one with whom I'm prepared to spend time.'

This simply spurred him on. He found it hard to sit still and she wondered what was happening in his trousers, horrified to think he might be getting an erection. She looked round her anxiously, but they were the only passengers at that end of the Pullman coach.

'You've never been in love?' he asked huskily, and his shoe rubbed against her sandal with an urgency she found disturbing.

'No.'

'Are you a virgin?'

Caitlin was left speechless at his audacity. She rose, picking up her bag and was about to head for the toilet to get away from him when the view gave way to streets, parks and houses as the train slowed down on the outskirts of Newquay.

She sank back in her seat, avoiding his eye, and he said, with such sincerity that she almost believed him, 'Forgive me. That was rude. It's just that you have such freshness and charm. I'm Rodney Cheyenne. Here's my card, and should you need anything, give me a ring. I live here and am an estate agent, in the property business.

Maybe you'll be looking to buy.'

'I think not, but thank you anyway,' she said, and tucked the card into her pocket.

She lost him when she stepped from the train. The station was busy and she handed in her ticket and walked towards the car park. There were several vehicles waiting to meet arrivals and she saw a bottle-green four-wheel drive with a placard stuck across the windscreen, reading, HIGH TIDES. FOR MISS COLBERT.

A man in his late twenties was lounging against the driver's door, smoking a roll-up. He was whiplash lean and wore baggy shorts, terrain sandals and a sleeveless vest. He was tanned so solidly that it was apparent he spent much time out of doors. His light-brown hair straggled to his shoulders from under a red bandanna that made him look like a pirate. He was clean-shaven, or would have been were it not for designer stubble. He spotted Caitlin, heaved his shoulders off the door and headed towards her.

'Are you Miss Colbert?' he asked laconically and, when she nodded, took her overnight bag and stowed it in the back. 'I'm Banan Driscol. I help out at High Tides . . . do a bit of driving for them, pick up customers, if they've come by train, organise sight-seeing trips. The rest of the time I'm working in my studio. I'm an artist.'

'That's interesting,' she said, making conversation, yet intrigued by this man. He seemed odd, unlike anyone she had met before. She climbed on to the bench seat beside him, and he drove off as if he was taking part in the Grand Prix, yet so competently that she was not alarmed.

'Tourists already,' he remarked conversationally.

'We locals call them emmets. Not that I flatter myself that I've been accepted. I've only been here six years and it takes a lifetime to become a true Cornishman, maybe more than that ... several generations. Have you been here before?'

'Ages ago,' Caitlin rejoined, failing to recognise any landmarks. Newquay was a typical holiday resort, as well as being a Mecca for the surfing enthusiasts. The north Atlantic rollers thundered up its shores and the wide crescent-shaped bay was ideal for the sport.

As Banan steered the FWD through the happily meandering crowds, she was on the edge of her seat with excitement, her breasts restricted by the belt. The gulls were now a reality, and the air was like wine, and there was that luminosity found nowhere but at the coast.

Like most resorts that had developed from the fishing industry, the narrow cobbled streets sloped down steeply to the harbour. Banan sailed effortlessly up a hill, coming out in an avenue between bungalows and holiday homes and boarding houses. They passed several caravan parks and took a side turning where a signpost proclaimed, QUEENSBURY 6 MILES.

Now the road wound and twisted, sharply down, then up again, like a switchback ride. At one moment they were shrouded by hedgerows thick with blossom, so steep and perilous that had they met another vehicle coming the other way one of them would have had to reverse, and in the next they were riding high. Then Caitlin wanted to cry out at the beauty of the spectacular scene spread far below the cliff road, where the trees were stunted and made almost perpendicular by the continual buffeting of the prevailing wind from the ocean.

'What a view,' she gasped, finding herself clinging to her seat.

He laughed and glanced sideways at her. 'Oh,
yes, and you haven't seen anything yet. Wait till we
drive by the Standing Stones. They're called the
Dancing Princesses. Some say there are twelve in
all, others come up with another figure. Apparently
they move, or so it is said. The story goes that in
pre-history, they were sisters who were turned into
stone by their wicked stepmother. Of course, the
archaeologists have them down as monoliths
erected by the ancient people who inhabited this
region. Whatever, they are grist to an artist's mill.
I've struggled to capture them in paint often, but
the light is always changing.'

And there they were, on Caitlin's left, between
the road and the cliff edge. Spread out in a ring,
they towered above the heather that lay like a
cloak over the turf, swirling and tossing in the
racing wind, purple mixed with golden gorse. She
leaned from the window and closed her eyes,
breathing in the scent of it, raising her face to the
warmth of the sun. She was achingly aware of
Banan beside her and the movements of his body
as he slowed down so that she might get the full
impact of the stones, saying, 'See how the sunlight
flickers over their grey surface, lightened by
patches of yellow lichen.'

Then he stopped the car but kept the engine
running. His arm rested along the back of the seat
and his breath whispered against her ear as he
said, 'Will you pose for me, Miss Colbert?'

Startled she turned to look at him, meeting his
hazel eyes with their incredibly long lashes, and

the smile that lifted his wide, humorous mouth. She could smell him, too, fresh sweat and body lotion, the clean, newly washed odour of his hair. His brown legs were shapely and muscular and he kept one foot on the accelerator, and his free hand on the wheel, but she didn't want to drive away. She longed to stay there with him, sharing that enchanted moment.

'Pose for you? I've never ... don't know if I'll have time,' she blurted out, but was aware that her panties were damp round the gusset and, more than anything, she wanted to feel the press of his firm lips on hers. 'I'm only here for the weekend.'

'But you'll be returning?' he insisted, and his hand closed over her shoulder with a pressure that could have been merely friendly or something more. 'I know why you're here. Belle gathered everyone together this afternoon and told us about you. Mary Macey's heir.'

'Did you know her?' She was looking at his knees and wondering if she dare lay a hand on the smooth, coppery skin.

'Yes. I got on with her fine. She appreciated art, and helped me out when times were hard. That's why I occasionally work for High Tides. I hope you don't sell up. I wouldn't like to see the old place go to strangers.'

'I don't know. I've never done anything like it before.' All Caitlin's fears and lack of confidence surfaced again and, responsive to her change of mood, Banan set the car in motion.

'You'll manage great,' he said comfortingly. 'You remind me of your aunt in some ways. Take the bull by the horns, baby. Give it a whirl, and pose for me sometime soon. I want you naked, of

41

course,' he added with a lift of his puckish eyebrows and a quirky grin.

Caitlin thought she would never stop blushing.

Leaving the stones behind, they followed the road that now descended between trees and was shortly augmented by picturesque cottages. 'These no longer belong to village people, but are mostly refurbished and used by townies as holiday lets or for their own spare time use with view to retirement,' said the informative Banan.

A bridge spanned a small bubbling river, and on the other side was the village green, surrounded by more houses, and with at least one pub and a supermarket. It had been kept in traditional style, a tourist attraction in summer, a typical clotted cream and scones, thatched roofs and strawberries hamlet where Americans and foreigners flocked with their cameras.

Banan drove through and they finally arrived in a quieter area, dominated by large houses set back in spacious gardens. Caitlin was almost crying now; Queensbury seemed so familiar. Banan swung into a drive, rumbled round a pond with a fountain set in the centre of a gravelled circle and braked below the wide steps that led to a doorway under a shell-shaped arch.

'Here we are,' he said, smiling at her, his lean, sun-browned hands resting on the wheel when she wanted them on her pussy. 'High Tides, ma'am, at your service – and so am I.'

CHAPTER

3

It was all coming back now, like the image from a black and white photo exposed long ago. Caitlin stared at the house. It had all the attributes of an Edwardian mansion, built in an era when a man put his wealth and achievements on display through his architecture, his women, the number of his servants. A place like this would have needed a live-in staff of at least twenty-five to cater for the needs of even a modest-sized family.

The frontage was impressive. Doric columns supported the arch, and there were tall sash windows on either side. It consisted of three storeys, with the addition of a basement below and attics under the eaves. A monkey-puzzle tree spread its branches on one side, and a Spanish chestnut on the other. Outbuildings and gardens lay behind it. Caitlin could see the glint of green-house roofs. The grounds were extensive, protected by high walls.

Banan escorted her up shallow stone steps to the imposing front door where light streamed through stained-glass panels. It opened immediately, and a woman was framed there. She came forward, hands outstretched, and Caitlin could see that she was a handsome lady between thirty and forty with a magnificent bosom. She was wearing a cream silk trouser suit, her highlighted hair styled in a casual, shaggy cut, and a wide smile on her generous poppy-red lips.

'Miss Colbert?' she carolled, bearing down on her in a cloud of heady French perfume. 'I'm so happy to meet you at last.'

'Please call me Caitlin.' It was heartening to receive such a warm welcome, though Caitlin found her almost overwhelming.

'Of course, and I'm Belle . . . Belle Godwin. My dear, how young you are, and how lovely,' the woman said, and ushered her inside.

'I'll leave you to it,' remarked Banan, dumping Caitlin's luggage on the polished parquet floor near the reception desk. 'I'll park the Range Rover round the back and pick up my van. Is there anything else you want doing today, Belle? No? Then I'll be off. Don't forget to visit my studio,' he added, winking at Caitlin in an intimate way that made it impossible to refuse. The naughty notion of taking off her clothes for him and posing naked made her nipples stiffen and caused mayhem in her cleft.

'He's gorgeous, isn't he?' said Belle, eyeing her shrewdly and linking an arm with hers as they walked through the hall. 'Our resident artist and oddball. The clients take to him at once; his manner is so easy and he knows a lot about local

44

history, so he is an ideal tour guide. But you'll learn all about him, and get to know the other people who work here. Including Barry,' she said, beckoning to a young man in a white shirt, a bow-tie and form-hugging black trousers who leapt to attention. 'This is Miss Colbert,' she said. 'See that Billy takes her bags to her apartment.'

'Yes, Mrs Godwin,' he answered deferentially, but there was a trace of impudence in his voice. He was a saucy person who wasn't in the least in awe of the manageress and jumped at the opportunity to pull rank on the bell-boy, a humble individual who was at the very bottom of the pecking order.

'Come to my office afterwards,' Belle added, bossily.

'Yes, Mrs Godwin. Certainly, madam.'

He stared boldly at Caitlin, and she was impressed by his wide shoulders and the way in which his back tapered to a V at the waist, the hollows in his flanks and his neat backside and the thick phallus lying against his inner left thigh.

My God, what's happening to me? she thought, panicking. I've never been so aware of sex before. Is it something in the air here? It was all getting too much. First the estate agent, then Banan and now Barry. Had all the personable men in Britain decamped for Cornwall?

Having given him his instructions, Belle ignored Barry. She sauntered across the hall and paused near an elevator, then pressed a button. The lift descended and the wrought-iron gates clanked open. 'I expect you'd like to freshen up before I take you on a tour of inspection. I've had Miss Macey's suite prepared for you.'

'Thank you,' Caitlin murmured, impressed by the old-fashioned ambience of the lift with its mahogany panels and bevel-edged mirrors. In fact the whole hotel, or what she had seen of it so far, seemed to exist in a time warp. Stepping into the elevator had been like becoming five again, except that she was no longer dwarfed by fittings, fixtures or adults.

'We're all very excited that you've come,' Belle went on, with enviable insouciance. 'There's so much to show you that I hardly know where to begin, so I've ordered dinner for two to be served in the restaurant. We can discuss things over the meal. I expect you'll be hungry after your journey. Then, later, I'll take you to the kitchens and introduce you to Raff Radley, our chef. He's a sometime TV personality when the powers-that-be decide to concentrate on the Cornish scene. It's very good for business.'

Caitlin was lost for words and, as they left the lift and passed along a corridor, she was even more impressed by High Tides grandeur. Thick carpets underfoot, tasteful seascapes in gilded frames hanging between wall-lamps with apricot silk shades, windows giving views of well-tended lawns and flowerbeds, a tennis court, a terrace with a swimming pool and padded loungers and round tables under big striped umbrellas. There was an atmosphere of comfort, not wildly extravagant but conveying an aura of luxury, nothing vulgar or cheap or tawdry, just old-fashioned, impeccable service where the customer was always right.

Belle stopped outside a pedimented cedar-wood door, slipped a key into the lock and turned it. She flicked a porcelain light switch and the sitting room sprang into life. 'There's everything you need here,' she explained, her eyes darting around in a proprietorial manner as if, indeed, the hotel belonged to her, not Caitlin.

'It's wonderful,' Caitlin exclaimed, impressed by the décor. This she definitely couldn't remember. Maybe she had never been taken to Aunt Mary's sanctum, or perhaps it had been changed since.

Yet it seemed to be genuine, straight from the period when the house was built. The lamps had opaque glass shades a lá Tiffany, and sumptuous balled and fringed curtains had been drawn across the bay windows. Fresh flowers were displayed in jardinières on carved pedestals. There was a buttoned Chesterfield and matching wing chairs, an escritoire, a china cabinet containing Stafford-shire figurines, and a marble fireplace with brass fittings. In complete contrast to these antiques, a 34-inch television with surround sound occupied a niche, along with a DVD and video player. Also the crème-de-la-crème of music centres, complete with racks of CDs.

Crikey, how could I not be comfortable here? Caitlin thought, as one after another of these treasures revealed themselves. Poor Mother. All she got was a painting. I wonder if it has been sent to her yet. I'll have to ask Belle, she's bound to know.

'This is the bedroom,' Belle said, with the flourish of a master-of-ceremonies whisking back stage curtains on a grand spectacle. She stood aside so that Caitlin might enter.

'Wow!' was all she could manage, staring in wonder and delight at the tester bed that domi-nated the room. It was hung with claret-coloured velvet drapes, and a lavish oriental throw spanned its width, while a heap of richly embroidered tapestry bolsters in jewel hues were piled against the inlaid headboard.

A gargantuan dressing table and an equally vast wardrobe matched the over-the-top bed. The fitted carpet had a red background with floral sprays, the wallpaper was an exotic vista of birds and lilies from the classic William Morris collection that was still popular after more than a hundred years.

'Miss Macey was an enthusiast. There was nothing she liked better than going to auction sales,' Belle said, watching Caitlin's reaction. 'I hope you share her impeccable taste. It would be a shame if High Tides was modernised – apart from the plumbing which is very up-to-date. Our patrons like it this way.'

'I shan't alter a thing,' Caitlin promised, almost too eagerly. She couldn't yet believe that all this belonged to her.

'You haven't planned what you're going to do? Keep it or sell it?' Belle asked, and Caitlin felt sorry for her. Of course she would be worried, fearing that she might lose her job and her home, for presumably she lived here, too.

'I want to see everything first, before I make up my mind,' Caitlin answered.

'It's a lot to take in, particularly if you've never done anything like it before,' Belle agreed, then opened a further door, saying, 'The bathroom. There are towels ... body lotion, shampoo. Just ring reception if there's anything you require. Dinner is at eight.'

'Thank you,' Caitlin said again, relieved when

Belle left and she could wander the suite on her own, easing herself into it as a cat let loose in a new home.

She was in love with the place, and wished there was someone she could phone to tell them all about it. But she certainly couldn't tell her mother. She wondered about Saskia, but decided it was better to talk to her in person when she returned to Granchester.

Confident that she was alone, she unpacked her bag and hung the few items of clothing in the wardrobe where they were immediately swallowed up. On an impulse, she had brought along the dress she had worn to Antonia's wine bar on that humiliating, frustrating and thwarting evening. It was either pack it or throw it away. She had the feeling it was jinxed, but had the urge to break the spell. Wearing it down to dinner in this marvellous place would surely prove good medicine. So far, still unable to believe this Cinderella story come true, she hadn't gone on a shopping spree, afraid to dip into her resources. She needed someone to guide her through the jungle of makeovers. This included clothes, re-vamping of her hair and general beauty treatment, which was what would be required if she was abandon the Plain Jane, schoolgirlish look in favour of that of a businesswoman.

Saskia sprang to mind again. How much she would enjoy spending lavishly on her friend's behalf, transforming the ugly duckling into a graceful swan. There was no one else Caitlin could turn to, except perhaps Belle Godwin, but she was older, and wouldn't have her finger on fashion's pulse like Saskia.

While Caitlin brooded on this, she spun the taps on the big, free-standing, claw-footed bath tub and started to undress, dropping each crumpled garment on to the floor. She caught sight of herself in the large mirror that filled one wall. Despite her weariness and high-strung state of anticipation and nervousness, she stood there and scrutinised herself. She always thought she looked better naked, her body and limbs forming a harmonious whole sometimes lacking when she wore the uninspired garments for which she usually settled. Some people had the knack for putting this with that, adding a scarf or a piece of junk jewellery and appearing chic and a million dollars. Not so Caitlin.

Nude she looked natural; her skin was faultless, her shoulders smooth, and her breasts firm yet full, with rosy-brown nipples that were now peaking in the sudden exposure. Small waist, rounded hips, the sweep of belly ending in a triangle of fair pubic curls, with a dark centre that shot down, straight as an arrow, to disappear between her legs. And these were pleasing, too, slender calves and ankles and feet with high arches and straight toes. She sighed as she ran her hands over her body, parting her thighs and dipping into her cleft, momentarily toying with her clit, then deciding to save that treat until she was in the bath.

She found a shower cap and tucked her hair inside, then stepped into the warm, scented water. The huge enamelled tub could have been a reproduction or an original put there when High Tides was built, or possibly later, purchased from a reclamation centre. Whatever: it was entirely in keeping. Big enough for two – but who would she

50

want to share it with? Banan? Maybe, or perhaps a dream hero she had yet to meet. Someone tall, dark and mysterious, nursing a terrible secret and needing her to help him. She was the first to admit that she had read too many Brontë novels in her impressionable teenage years, yearning for a Heathcliff or a Mr Rochester.

Oh, get real! her sensible self insisted. They'd be impossible; macho and chauvinistic. You'd hate them in real life, and they'd know nothing about the clit, convinced that all you need to sweep you to bliss is their penis and their orgasm.

She sank into the water, lay back and rested her head against the scrolled edge. The foam frothed, covering all of her except the pink tips of her nipples and her curling pubic fronds. She stretched her legs, and wavelets rolled up towards her dimpled navel and played round her bottom like lascivious little fingers. She moaned and reached down to part her labial wings and locate her swollen bud.

Now she could play with it, enjoy a leisurely wank before the trials and tribulations of the evening ahead. There was nothing so comforting as bringing oneself to climax. Who needed men really? Only as a means to produce children and even this was no longer essential, what with test-tubes and frozen sperm. She had heard of at least one lesbian couple who had become parents through the simple use of a turkey baster and a donation from a male friend.

But these ideas did not fulfil the romantic that still lurked in Caitlin's heart. She daydreamed of a white wedding and, in due course, a family of cherubic and perfectly behaved children. She was a pushover for bride magazines, Mothercare and Baby Gap. She pushed these thoughts away, concentrating instead on self-induced pleasure, rubbing her soapy nipples with one hand and feeling the echo of sensation in her clit.

She parted her legs a little and lifted her hips. The water slid away, exposing that delicate bush, and she ran her fingertips over the darkened whorls, then, abandoning her breasts, held the labial lips apart and stretched her clit higher, making it stand away from its cowl. She squinted down at it, proud of its size, that well-defined little organ with no purpose other than pleasure, and blessing the day she had discovered it, quite by chance, when in her teens.

Oh, it was exquisite! She had meant to make it last, but once she began to fondle it, first rubbing it each side, then back towards its root somewhere deep in her pubis, she found it difficult to stop. Moaning, lids lowered, she blanked out all thoughts save the delightful sensations in her wonderful bud. She wanted to show it to someone, and created a scenario in which she had an appointment with a gynaecologist, and he was begging her to permit him to display her clit to a party of medical students.

'Please, Miss Colbert,' he said, so suave and beguiling, a famous man in his field who was actually pleading with her to show off her assets. 'Yours is the most perfect clitoris I've yet seen. It's so large, and responds so well. May I call in my pupils?'

'Yes,' Caitlin answered, almost coming as he continued to praise her nubbin.

They entered, a mixed bag of white-coated

males and females, all eager to learn from the great man. 'I want two of you to stand at her head and caress her nipples,' he ordered, in an excitingly brisk and masterly fashion. They did and it was heavenly. He moved till he was standing at the foot of the examination couch, easing her down till her legs embraced his thighs. 'That pillow under her hips, if you please,' he snapped, and it was done. He was staring straight at her wet and gaping cleft.

'Come closer,' he advised his students and they bent over, gazing at her pudenda. 'Do you see the clitoris? It stands out like the head of a penis, rising from its foreskin that is formed by the labia. It's a remarkable organ, a bundle of erectile tissue, supersensitive to stimulation, far more so than the penis which, in comparison, is a dull thing. Yet it has to be fondled gently, and prefers to be slippery with the woman's juices or spittle or lubricating gel though, on occasions, it can respond to a harsh, dry rubbing. Miss Colbert is very wet, and I'm going to spread some of her fluid up and over her clit. Keep caressing her nipples and I think, we shall have a result within a few seconds.'

'Oh, yes . . . *yes!*' Caitlin moaned aloud.

Now fantasy gave way to reality – the reality of her own favourite middle digit flying over that hard, pealike gem. It throbbed and ached, the agonising pleasure rising and rising till it peaked and she cried out in her extremity. She clasped her mound, brought herself down gently, finger still in place. And she wanted to do it again, keep up the pressure, rub and rub and rub till the clit was ready to give up its wonders once more. When she was in the mood, she could climax again and again and, feeling elated, knew that this might be the occasion. But no. She had things to do. Later, when she finally retired for the night, she could bring herself to repeated ecstasy.

She took up the sponge and started to soap her breasts and cleft, lathering her skin in scented suds. And this hotel is mine ... *all mine* ... she thought, and clasped her fork with the sheer joy of it. A touch, and she was off again, rousing her pink pearl and unable to stop until another orgasm shuddered through her and she collapsed back in the bathtub.

Belle was seated in a computer operator's chair in her office. She took a sip at the brandy glass in her hand, licking her lips in appreciation of the fine vintage. Nothing but the best had been hers over the months since Mary's demise. As for her heir? A nice girl, Belle decided, and wished her no harm, but she recognised that Caitlin was green as grass and that she, Belle, could influence her whichever way she liked.

She leaned forward and, at the touch of a button, a bank of TV monitors lit up. Closed-circuit cameras had been installed several years before after a series of break-ins. High Tides was too full of costly items, to say nothing of the property of guests, to put at risk. Cameras were high profile around the house, grounds, kitchens and in every public room. These had successfully put paid to the attentions of organised villains and light-fingered opportunists alike.

Mary had strictly forbidden any invasion of her guests' privacy. Sometimes Belle regretted this, as now, when she might have spied on Caitlin. The thought of so doing excited her, and she slid out of her silk trousers and panties, hooking a leg over each chair arm, her delta parting, smooth and glistening between lips that were fringed by hair much darker than that on her head. She wasn't a natural blonde.

Ah, these peaceful moments when, incarcerated in her office having given orders not to be interrupted, she worked on the computer, the organisation of High Tides entirely in her hands. Knowledge was power and she shared the hotel's financial secrets with no one save her accountant. It also gave her this precious time for relaxation, so valuable in her busy life, where she could daydream about fit young men and excite herself to orgasm, if she felt inclined.

Her busy finger with its scarlet lacquered nail, worked around her clit, the labial wings swelling, the nub engorging, her heart hammering with anticipation. She opened her blouse and touched the crimped nipples with her free hand. They looked like strawberries among the white foam of her lacy bra. She imagined running her palms over Barry's body, exploring every hollow and peak. She wetted her full lower lip and could almost taste his sexual juices, wanting to suck him into her mouth, and flick her tongue tip over his fat, pulsating cock.

Her movements were faster now. She was rapidly losing control, her clit thrumming with the white heat of desire. She moaned and flung back her head, her face distorted as she came. Her womb contracted and the tight coil inside her relieved itself in a vast, annihilating spasm of intense and violent pleasure.

'Ah . . . ah . . .' she groaned, unable to restrain herself.

A tap on the door and, 'Are you there, madam?' said Barry from outside.

She killed the screen, and swivelled the chair so that she faced him when he entered. He'd get the tantalising sight of her splayed legs and wet, swollen pussy, and would preen himself, convinced that it was all to do with him and his cock.

'Don't you know I'm not to be disturbed?' she teased, then added, 'Come in, Barry. Lock the door after you, and get your trousers off.'

He had arrived at just the right moment, and her heart softened towards this impudent young stud. He was so easy to manipulate, awed by her sexual experience and position of command. And she needed a large male tool, wanted that bar of flesh to fill her cunt and give her inner muscles something to grip round. There was plenty of time before her dinner engagement with Caitlin, whose innocence was proving to be an interesting challenge.

'And this is Raff, our chef,' said Belle proudly. 'Raff, meet Miss Colbert, who now owns High Tides.'

They had just entered a brightly lit room dominated by big stainless steel tables and work surfaces. There were ovens, refrigerators, dishwashers, racks of utensils, pans, pots, skillets and an awesome variety of knives, choppers, sieves and whisks. Raff's minions were tidying up, and he watched them with an eagle eye, a demon when it came to cleanliness. In fact, they seemed so scared that Caitlin suspected him of being an absolute tyrant, and trembled at the idea of working under him. Thank God, she would never have to.

He was a great bull of a man, his body thickset and hairy, from what she could see of his mighty arms and the chest that showed at the unbuttoned neck of his overall. He had black hair, cut short and mostly hidden under a white cap, and his eyes were black, too, peering at her with an interest that practically amounted to a leer as he lingered on her breasts, exposed by that spangled green dress. She thought he might be of foreign extraction, but when he spoke his accent was pure Cockney. Not a local, then, so what was he doing in Cornwall?

Caitlin didn't know quite what to say to him. How do you address the man who has just been responsible for the most memorable meal you have ever eaten? All evening she had been embarrassed every time Belle introduced her to members of staff, from grumpy old Mr Ramsey who seemed to hold the position that a head butler might have had in the old days, to the most lowly of the kitchen crew. But the chef – that was something else. She'd watched enough television cookery programmes to know that he ruled the roost.

'I'm pleased to meet you,' she said and he took her hand in a fist like a side of bacon.

'The pleasure's all mine,' he said, stepping closer, his breath perfumed with spices, for he was chewing on something exotic – cloves or cardamom or cinnamon bark. 'I trust that you enjoyed your meal.'

'It was perfect,' she exclaimed, and meant it.

His eyes crinkled at the outer corners and his smile widened and she realised that he was not only extremely talented in the culinary arts, but was also an attractive man. If I lived with him, I'd never have to worry about meals again, she thought incongruously.

It seemed he never stopped. Even now, he was subjecting her to only three-quarters of his attention as he was standing by the hob, stirring a sauce, sniffing and tasting, presumably about to partake of his own supper now that the restaurant was closed.

'Have you been down here before, Miss Colbert?' he asked, and now he was leaning with his back against one of the sinks, his hips thrust forward, the apron tied round his waist, his long, strong legs in white trousers crossed at the ankles. He regarded her with an interest that was more than that of an employee towards the boss.

'When I was a child.'

'And you're planning to stay?'

'Possibly.'

'She's only just arrived,' Belle put in. 'Plenty to see and plenty to do. If you're done here, Caitlin, I suggest it's getting on for bedtime. Another day, another deed tomorrow.'

'Feel free to come into my kitchen any time,' Raff said, and it was as if he had stepped even closer, though he hadn't moved a muscle. 'Are you interested in cookery?'

'I used to join in classes at school.'

Not for the first time that night she wished Belle wasn't there, aware that she was observing her closely, as if assessing her ability with the staff. Perhaps she was wondering if she was going to prove so able that she would eventually take over, leaving her high and dry.

'It's an art,' he replied smugly, and now he was

looking at the shadowy outline of her legs and the dip between them where her thighs divided. 'Some are born masters, others acquire the skills. It reads across the board . . . taste, textures, smells . . . as potent as sex, Miss Colbert. Don't you agree?'

'I've never looked at it that way,' she said, her cheeks flushing with more than the heat from the stove.

He lowered his voice and said, 'Let me teach you.' He leaned forward and murmured in her ear, 'I want to spread cream over your body and then lick it off, slowly. I'd like to put ice-cubes on your nipples, just to see them peak, and trickle chocolate sauce over your cunny and then clean up every crack. My tongue is well trained. I'd love to slurp at your clit.'

Red as fire, Caitlin broke away. 'Good night, Raff,' she said breathlessly, already halfway towards the door.

Belle caught up with her, saying, 'What was all that about? I couldn't hear.'

'Oh, nothing,' Caitlin lied, her pussy aching, dew dampening her panties. 'He was just offering to show me one of his secret recipes.'

'Oh?' Belle looked doubtful, then added, 'Don't take him too seriously, my dear. He loves to tease. Food and women are his passion. Shall we go into the bar? Do you fancy a nightcap?'

Caitlin wanted to go to bed to review the events of the day. She still couldn't get over the décor of the restaurant, or the apparent affluence of the clientele. Belle had talked and talked during the meal, and Caitlin's head was buzzing with information. There was so much to learn and . . . steady on there . . . she warned herself, you're going on as if you've already made up your mind to move down here and keep High Tides.

The bar was almost empty, all subdued lighting and soft, jazzy music with a sobbing saxophone, like something from a 1940s movie. *Fill 'em up, Joe. That's one for my baby, and one more for the road.*

She accepted a gin and tonic, simply because she didn't know what else to order. It was a double, and she and Belle perched on stools and chatted to the bartender, at least Belle did, after announcing yet again that Caitlin had stepped into Miss Macey's shoes. Caitlin was uncomfortably aware of how the staff's attitude changed once they realised who she was. It wasn't exactly deference they exuded, more a kind of wariness, as if suddenly being put on their best behaviour lest she sack them. It wasn't a happy position to be in, but she knew she'd have to get used to it if she was going to be the one doing the hiring and firing.

She got to her room around midnight and undressed quickly, dying to jump into bed, but as she stood there naked before reaching for her blue nightshirt with its Tigger motif, she heard a sound. She looked across the room sharply. There it was again. Someone in the garden was throwing pebbles up at the window. She crept over and twitched back a corner of the heavy curtains. The moonlight outside washed everything with a blue-white brilliance, bright as day. She lifted the sash and leaned out.

'Who's there?' she called tremulously.

'It's me, Banan,' he said, keeping his voice low.

'What do you want at this unearthly hour?'

'Meet me down here early in the morning. Before you get embroiled with business discussions with

Belle. Come to my studio for breakfast.'

She was tempted to turn chicken and refuse, but a sudden, new-found surge of confidence made her say, 'All right,' and she pressed her bare breasts against the sill as she leaned out, feeling her nipples harden and seeing the pale wedge of his face upturned towards her.

'That's my girl,' he chortled. 'I want to be the one to show you the wonders of Queensbury, to say nothing of doing your portrait. I'll meet you here around seven-thirty. OK?'

'OK,' she whispered, and he disappeared into the darkness of the trees.

Thrilled by having already made an assignation when she'd not been there for more than six hours, she cleaned her teeth and then jumped into the vastness of the bed. She left the reading light on and thumbed through a magazine, but soon she became accustomed to the softness of the mattress and the newness of her surroundings. She had promised herself another climax, but felt too sleepy, merely folding her hand round her mound as she lay on her side and snuggled into the pillows. Tomorrow she would see Banan. Now it was time to sleep and wake refreshed, ready to face whatever the new day might bring.

'There's gossip running rife in the village, sir,' said the wiry, dark-suited man, his movements neat and precise, his bearing suggesting that he had once been in the army.

His hair was sandy, short and swept back, and his face was thin, with finely chiselled features, his expression respectful as he laid out his employer's riding breeches and hacking jacket. Contrary to custom, these were neither beige nor tweed but black and he approved of this, and of the tidiness of the bedroom, for he disliked clutter above all things.

'Indeed, Robert,' replied Tristan Trevellyan, sparing him hardly a glance as he carried his cup of strong café noir to the mullioned window and looked out on the garden, seeing but not seeing the rose bushes, the parterre, the maze. 'D'you mean to say they've found a topic other than myself, on which to feed their malicious imaginations?'

'It seems so, sir,' Robert replied, stroking a hand over the black T-shirt that Tristan would wear next to his skin. 'Apparently, Miss Macey's heir arrived at High Tides yesterday.'

'Ah, that would set tongues wagging,' Tristan said sardonically. 'And who or what is this fortunate beneficiary?'

'A young woman, by the name of Caitlin Colbert. Miss Macey's great-niece.'

Tristan frowned. He had just stepped out of the shower and was wearing a towel knotted round his hips. A striking man in his mid-thirties, he was tall and rangy, his raven hair rendered darker by the water, and straggling over the nape of his neck.

He didn't take kindly to any change in his routine or environment. There had been more than enough of that when Portia had vanished like the will-o'-the-wisp she was. Eventually the police had left him in peace, though letting it be known that the case was not closed or their inquiries over.

All this had grievously harmed his standing in the area. The last in a long line of landowners, he still received a handsome income from farms and various other agricultural ventures in Devon and

Cornwall, plus interests in the north of England and sensibly invested stocks and shares. Something of a recluse, he had been brought out of himself when he married Portia. She was very popular, beautiful and with a talent for giving lavish parties and throwing herself into village events, the life and soul of every gathering. People loved her – and so had he.

His scowl darkened, and Robert kept his peace, recognising the storm signals. 'I can manage,' Tristan said brusquely. 'Tell Keith to saddle Merlin.'

'Breakfast, sir?'

'On my return.'

When Robert had gone, rather reluctantly, Tristan thought, no doubt wanting to talk more of Miss Macey's heir, he dressed swiftly, stamping his feet down into his riding boots. Then he ran a comb through his hair and a hand over his freshly shaven jaw, picked up his crop and strode from the bedroom. He ran lightly down the grand staircase into the Great Hall and out into the crisp morning air. He took deep breaths, trying to dispel the gloom that any reminder of Portia always brought.

It was better in the stable where his stallion was waiting, tossing his black mane, flecks of sunlight dancing like diamond dust over his ebony coat. Saddled-up and riding away from the house, Tristan headed towards the coast. The mention of a stranger had put his hackles up and he felt it his duty to investigate, just as one of his ancestors might have done at the rumoured arrival of free-booters or marauding Vikings. He smiled grimly; this was far-fetched, of course, but somehow he never had got used to visitors in the area, even though they brought prosperity, and the idea of High Tides being taken over was repugnant to him. Not that he ventured into Queensbury often, but he resented anything that upset the status quo.

'What a place! What a view!' Caitlin enthused, running over the firm wet sand, digging in her toes and venturing to where the small waves frolicked up the beach.

It was stunning; a wide bay enclosed by a semi-circle of rugged cliffs. She and Banan had reached it by climbing down a winding path bordered by sea-pinks and marram grass that clung tenuously to the sandy soil. Caitlin had touched them and the soft, feathery tamarisk as she passed, lifting her fingers to her nose and inhaling the smell of crushed foliage, remembering Raff, master of the kitchens. The wind had lifted her hair, and broad bands of sunlight had broken from rifts in the clouds, moving radiantly over the vista of sea and rocks and rolling dunes.

She knew that part of the enchantment was due to Banan who, true to his word, had met her in the garden and escorted her through a copse and down to a secluded cottage overlooking the bay. There, in the barn that he had converted into a studio-cum-living room, he had fed her on coffee and buttered rolls and freshly smoked mackerel and fruit. She had never felt so light-hearted and easy in a man's company. He let her know that he wanted her, but there was no pressure. He was pacing himself to her. And this had the desired effect of making her wish he'd do something about it. She didn't want to rush things but found herself leaning into him as they sat side by side on his battered, sagging settee.

He had become serious then, and his arm had tightened about her and he had kissed her in a way that made her melt inside and want more and more. It was he who had released her mouth, and suggested that they visit the cove. 'We have all day,' he had said. 'And all night, if you want.'

'I do want,' she had confessed.

'What about Belle?' he had reminded.

'Time enough for her and work and the accountant and God knows what else. What about me?' she had protested.

Now they were like two children playing truant from school, and Banan leapt and pranced and turned cartwheels for her benefit. He was wearing denim cut-offs, short and tight and with frayed hems that clasped his strong, brown thighs and pushed his bulge into prominence. He discarded his sleeveless vest and his torso was as brown as his legs, his chest practically bare of hair, except for tiny circles round his wine-red nipples. He wasn't overdeveloped, like someone who worked out, but looked strong and she liked the way the waistband of his shorts dipped below his navel as he moved, and the salty smell of his skin when he slung an arm over her shoulders as they splashed through the shallows.

She wished she had worn something more daring than the sensible, knee-length hiking shorts that were all she owned. Baggy, beige and serviceable, she wished she had the nerve to buy something briefer, as brief as those worn by popstars, which would display her bottom and press into her crack, outlining her plump labia. I will, she resolved. I'll go shopping and look for some.

Then, suddenly, her attention was riveted on a horseman who appeared at the far end of the beach. He had materialised without warning. At one moment there was no sign of him and, in the next, he was bearing down on them, sand and sea spraying from beneath his horse's thudding hooves.

'Where did he come from?' Caitlin asked, grasping Banan's arm, a bolt of fear shooting through her.

'He rounded the headland from the next cove,' he answered, staring at the rider from under frowning brows. 'It's easy enough to do when the tide is low, though impassable when it's not. You have to be careful to watch the tides or you'll get cut off.'

They had automatically stopped, up to their ankles in sea and shingle. Nearer the horseman came, and nearer, and it looked as if he intended to trample them, but at the last minute he swerved and hauled on the reins, his foam-flecked horse blowing down its nose, rolling its eyes and throwing back its noble head.

No one spoke, and Caitlin could do nothing but stare at the stranger, unable to look away as his eyes met hers, met and held them, and she was possessed of a strange sense of déjà-vu, though convinced that she had never seen him before. He rode his stallion like an emperor, a striking figure, his big hands controlling the restless beast. She guessed he would be over six feet tall, and the black jacket and breeches echoed the colour of his shoulder-length hair. His face was expressionless, his sea-grey, steely eyes boring into hers. Her heart pounded and her loins yearned, for he was unfairly handsome, his cheekbones high and pronounced, and he had an aquiline profile that had the untamed, threatening beauty of a hawk.

Then without speaking he broke the spell, digging his heels into his mount's sides so that it reared and took flight, quickly disappearing among the mighty heaps of tumbled rocks and heading for the next bay.

'And who was that?' Caitlin gasped, shading her eyes with her hand and trying to catch another glimpse of him.

Banan gave a quirky smile, shrugged and said, 'That, O best beloved, was Tristan Trevellyan who owns most of the area. Three hundred years ago he would have been the feudal lord, and still likes to behave as if he is. He lives between Queensbury and Porthjude, in his ancestral pile, part fortress, part Tudor mansion. It's called Lyons Court. He is an unsociable bugger. He doesn't like strangers and keeps much to himself. I know him because he commissioned me to paint a portrait when I first arrived here. It was of his wife, before she disappeared. She's never been found, vanished into thin air, and rumour has it that he killed her.'

CHAPTER

4

It had been hard saying goodbye to Banan, even though the parting was to be of short duration. Caitlin was thankful that she hadn't slept with him, and grateful that he hadn't pushed it; he was content, it seemed, to be her companion when she could escape from Belle, Raff, Mr Ramsey and the daily lessons in keeping a hotel running smoothly.

She listened and learned and made copious notes, visiting the storerooms, the linen cupboards, the wine cellars, the grounds and those who maintained them, also the Truro warehouses that supplied everything from breakfast cereals to toilet-rolls. The economics of bulk buying were explained to her in detail. The accountant duly arrived, settled himself in Belle's office, took over her computer and punched in finance data. High Tides was flourishing and showed a substantial profit margin.

By now Caitlin had decided. In for a penny, in for a pound, she was going to keep the hotel.

'You'll stay on, Belle, won't you?' she had begged, when making her intentions known. 'I couldn't manage without you, and I don't want a single thing changed. You'll have to be patient with me. I know it'll be hard going to begin with, but I'm sure I'll get the hang of it eventually.'

Belle hugged her, and promised to do all she could and Caitlin left for Granchester in a new, top-of-the-range car that Mary had bought but never used. Caitlin produced her licence and ownership was transferred to her. There was no time for her to brush up with a professional driving instructor. She had made do with Banan, taking the wheel and making several trips to Newquay and braving the steep, winding coastal roads under his guidance.

Midweek she went back to Armstrong Lodge to sort through her things and decide what to throw out and what to dispatch to Cornwall.

The first person she met was Saskia.

'Hi, stranger! Where have you been?' Saskia asked, planting herself in the hall, legs braced in a pair of kinky mules with thick transparent plastic soles and high rainbow heels.

These, along with her patchwork denim miniskirt, made her look taller, slimmer, even more sexy. It was designer-constructed from bits of old jeans that should have been consigned to the ragbag; Saskia had paid a penny short of one hundred pounds for it.

'Away,' Caitlin replied, aware that Saskia had no intention of letting her get to the stairs until her curiosity had been satisfied.

'*No!*' Saskia expressed scornful disbelief. 'And I thought you were sulking in your room. Of course, you've been away. I can see that by your tan. And where is this "away"?'

'Cornwall,' Caitlin said, then made up her mind to come clean. 'Look, there's something I want you to know. Come up to my room.'

'I thought you'd never ask,' Saskia replied archly, sashaying ahead of her.

It was stuffy inside, and Caitlin threw open the window, already missing the sea air. She couldn't wait to get back. 'Sit down,' she said. 'Sorry I can't offer you a coffee or anything. I'm out of supplies.'

Saskia coiled voluptuously on the couch, observing Caitlin and saying, 'I had the feeling you'd never speak to me again after the mess with Tom. Is that why you've been lying low?'

'No,' Caitlin answered, casting her eye round the rented bedsit that seemed even smaller, more dreary and dilapidated after the glories of High Tides.

'I was only trying to bring you out of yourself,' Saskia explained, fishing in her enormous and fashionable tote bag and unearthing cigarettes and a lighter. 'But I realised that it wasn't going to work with you and him.'

'It doesn't matter. It's all in the past. I'm moving on now. Let me explain, but promise you won't freak,' Caitlin began, and by the time she had finished, Saskia was rigid, cigarette burning itself out in the ashtray.

'Let me get this straight,' she said, when Caitlin paused for breath. 'You've come into money. Is this a wind up? You're not joking, are you?'

'Would I? It's true. Oh, Saskia, you should see

the hotel! You must come and stay. Say you will.'

'I'm not a seaside kind of a gal,' she protested, laughing. 'Can you see me with a bucket and spade?'

'It's not like that. I've a pool and everything. You should meet the guys. There's Banan the artist, and Raff the chef and I haven't even begun to trawl for other talent, though there was a man on the train . . . an estate agent called Rodney. I met the lord of the manor a few days ago, and he's a hunk, sinister and scary, and Banan says his wife disappeared under mysterious circumstances. It's all happening. I'm sure that Belle Godwin is bonking a waiter called Barry, and he must be twenty years her junior.'

'Slow down. OK, so I'm convinced. Queensbury is a hotbed of sin, and you're rolling in loot now, like winning the Lottery.'

'Something like that.'

'And you're leaving here and going back for good?'

'As soon as I can.'

'What about graduation day?'

'I don't give a monkey's. They can send me my diploma.'

Saskia gave her a long, searching look. 'You've changed,' she said. 'Is it the men or the cash?'

'A little of both, I guess,' said Caitlin, pushing back a lock of hair that had fallen over her forehead. She was aware of the alteration that had already taken place within her. She now viewed Saskia as an equal, knowing that she could do whatever she liked – change her image, dye her hair green, walk around half naked or remain as she was. Spend or save, go where she would and with whom.

'Are you going to say goodbye to the gang? Shall we meet up in Antonia's tonight?'

Caitlin shook her head. 'I've no real friends here, apart from you, and can't wait to leave. All I have to do is go through my belongings, chuck out most of them and hire a man and a van to take the rest to High Tides. My car's not big enough.'

'You've a car?'

'A Mercedes.'

'Nice one. That's it then, is it?' Saskia said, getting to her feet, and there was a finality about their parting that bothered Caitlin.

'Here's my address and phone number, my mobile as well.' Caitlin pulled a card from her jacket pocket. 'Let me have yours and we'll keep in touch. I really *do* want you to visit.'

'I'm moving to London at the end of the month. Dad's found me a flat in a groovy converted warehouse in Docklands, and I'm starting work on interiors with one of Mum's friends. I'll send you my address and landline number. You already know my mobile number.'

Caitlin walked with her to the door and they embraced awkwardly, though she was all too aware of Saskia's svelte body under that silly skirt and skimpy top. Once, she had been more than a little afraid and embarrassed at the slightest indication that their friendship might spill over into passion. Now, the thought no longer appalled her. She was missing Banan, though their relationship had barely got off the ground. The notion of falling on to the settee with Saskia, and pinching her pert breasts had a certain, forbidden fascination. She wanted to go further, rucking up her skirt and finding the tanga that hardly hid her mound and

72

playing with that sensitive niche between her love lips.

Saskia was looking at her with knowing eyes, one brow raised questioningly. Caitlin blushed, turned what might have been a lover's embrace into a quick squeeze, then let her go.

'This isn't over, you know,' Saskia said, and reached out a finger to caress Caitlin's lips. 'I'll be down to High Tides as soon as I can. Keep in touch, and watch out for the men. Can you be sure they are after you and not your money? Are you still looking for Mr Right?'

'I suppose I am,' Caitlin replied, guardedly.

'No such creature exists. If and when I finally decide to marry, then I'll settle for Mr Trainable,' was Saskia's last shot.

'Are you ready for this?' Banan asked as Caitlin mounted the dais under the great north-facing skylight.

'Ready as I'll ever be,' she answered, as nervous as a kitten and seriously questioning the wisdom of agreeing to pose for him.

Hardly giving her breathing space, he'd been on her case as soon as she got back. Was it true that absence makes the heart grow fonder? she mused. He had hung around impatiently while she moved her baggage in and took up residence in the master suite. Then there was Belle monopolising her time, and dinner and a visit to Raff's domain where he flirted with her outrageously, and then finally Banan managed a quiet word, not exactly asking, more demanding that she be at the studio in the morning.

His impetuosity was arousing, and she had

parted her lips for his kiss when they said good-night. He had held her close and she had felt the hardness of his cock through his cotton shorts and her dirndl skirt. She had wormed her hand down between them and closed it round his straining tool. He had groaned into her mouth and she had been sorely tempted to invite him to stay, but was even more wary, remembering Saskia's warning.

Now the tension was palpable; she knew and so did he that she wouldn't leave until they had made love. 'Take off your dressing gown, and lean against that pillar,' he said, fiddling with his palette and brushes and a large canvas propped on an easel.

The moment of truth, and she had never been more self-conscious. She opened the silk kimono that he had provided, and slid it down to her waist. Banan did not look at her and, a trifle miffed, she dropped the remaining covering and tossed it over the back of a chair. The pillar was in the Doric style, a polystyrene stage prop, broken off to just above waist height. Caitlin leaned against it. Banan looked up.

'Put one arm on it. That's right, reach across. Nice . . . nice . . . sort of sink into it and look wistful . . . no, not wistful . . . lustful, as if you're fantasising about sex. Eyes sultry. Lips pouting. Good. One hand on your tits. Lovely. I'm going to take some snaps so that I can work on it when you're not here, OK?'

'OK,' she muttered. He hadn't said anything about photographs. There was nothing to stop him passing them round in the pub. All she had to rely on was his word not to act the cad, and his professionalism that would make him keep the tricks of the trade up his sleeve.

She started like a frightened doe when he stepped up beside her, took her forearm in his thin fingers and adjusted the pose. 'What am I supposed to represent?' she asked for something to say, anything to ignore the tingling sensation that shot from her loins to her core at his merest touch.

He shrugged and pointed to several pictures that hung against the wooden walls. They were ethereal, possessing a hypnotic, dreamlike quality. The sea in all its moods: stormy and grey, sun-washed, moon washed, pale and misty blue. There were eldrich horses plunging through the spume, ghostly, uncanny, and fairy women, too, naked and alluring, but pale as death apart from scarlet lips. They reminded Caitlin of Dracula's vampire brides.

'Do you sell many of these?' she asked, restraining the impulse to lean into him instead of the pillar.

'I don't do too badly, especially in the tourist season. A gallery in St Ives shows them for me, and we're planning an exhibition in London next winter.'

'Are they expensive?'

'Not for what they are,' he said. There was no false modesty about him. 'They range from a thousand pounds upwards.'

'Would you be offended if I bought one for High Tides? There's a noticeable gap in the hall where a Highland scene took pride of place. Miss Macey left it to my mother, purely to aggravate her, I suspect, for she hated that picture.'

'Would you like the one of you that I'm about to do?' he asked, admiring her with an artist's eye and a man's desire.

'Maybe not. I wouldn't want the guests making comparisons and guessing it was the proprietress skinny-dipping. I'll settle for the sea horses,' she answered, then took the chance of opening the subject that had been tantalising her for days. 'Did you say that you painted a picture of Tristan Trevellyan's wife?' she asked, but casually, as if it was of no real interest to her.

'That's right.' He seemed more concerned in tucking a strand of her hair away from her shoulder, making her shiver as the back of his hand brushed her nipple.

'What was she like?'

'Beautiful. Probably the most beautiful woman I have ever seen.'

Caitlin experienced a twinge of jealousy. How dare he find anyone more beautiful than herself? This was childish and she knew it, saying, 'And where is the portrait now?'

'I delivered it to Lyons Court and supervised it being hung in the Long Gallery. I presume it is still there.'

'But you said she disappeared. How? What happened?'

He shrugged and left the dais, concentrating on the canvas that was blank apart from a background of foggy trees. 'No one knows. Tristan was besotted with her, but she was flighty whereas he's a studious bloke. Maybe she was having an affair. She even came on to me.'

'And did you respond?' Caitlin was starting to dislike Portia.

He grinned and pulled a face. 'I don't think that's any of your business, Miss Colbert. Anyway, it was years ago. Then she vanished without trace

– there one day and gone the next. Tristan was the prime suspect. Nothing was ever proved, but mud sticks.'

'Do you think he murdered her?' Cold fingers crawled down Caitlin's spine and it was nothing to do with her exposure.

'I don't know. I wouldn't have thought so, for he was very much in love with her. She wound him round her little finger. But maybe she did something that pushed him over the edge.' His eyes cut to her and he added, 'Why are you so interested?'

'I'm not really, but want to get to know Queensbury and its inhabitants. He appears to be an important person.'

'Oh, I can fill you in about most folk here, a mine of information, me. What d'you want to know? Who's bonking who?' He laughed, then talked non-stop as he used charcoal to outline her figure on the canvas before mixing colours and laying them on with sure strokes.

Caitlin listened and digested the facts, and the time passed swiftly as she held the pose and Banan worked like a fury. During the first rest period, he wrapped her in the Japanese robe and brought her hot coffee. She was stiff, realising that being an artist's model was no sinecure – it was surprisingly hard work.

The second rest found them lingering on the dais, neither eager to start again. It was noon, and the sun was high, the air still and hot, even inside. 'We should take a swim,' Banan suggested, but he did not move, his arm round her waist, paint smeared fingers seeking her curves beneath the kimono. He suddenly lost control, pushing it away, his eyes glittering and his voice harsh as he exclaimed, 'It's no good, Caitlin. I've got to fuck you. Say you want me, too.'

His hands were paddling over her breasts, and his penis was pushed against her pubis and she gasped, visions of Saskia's stern face obliterated by the heat spiralling up from her core. 'I want you,' she confessed.

He sank to his knees between her legs, parted her labia and licked her clit. She clung to his shoulders and then his head, burying her fingers in his tousled hair, smelling oil paint and turpentine and holding him there as she rode his tongue to climax. She shuddered, came, sank to the faded carpet covering the dais and Banan released his cock from the fly of his threadbare jeans and it was all she had hoped for, eight inches of meaty flesh, thicker than she had expected. He wasn't circumcised, his foreskin rolled back from the shining, fiery dome. His balls were big, luscious globes dangling behind his penis. She reached for him, took that impressive baton in hand and rubbed till he drew back.

'Stop, before I shoot all over you,' he gasped, then fumbled in his pocket for a condom.

She was pleased that he was so thoughtful, yet a trifle insulted because he had been prepared, expecting her to give in to him. But this lasted only a second and then she lay on her back and opened wide, resting her ankles on his shoulders, as he pushed off his jeans and lowered himself, guiding his latex-shrouded cock into her.

Just for a chilling moment, she wondered if that was it. Did he intend to work his penis in and out until he climaxed, expecting her to come simultaneously? The size of him filling her up, the pressure of his glans butting against her cervix, was thrilling but frustrating. She gripped him with her inner muscles, but knew she'd never climax that way. G-Spot? She doubted its existence. It was her clitoris that needed stimulating again, one orgasm never enough for her. She wondered if she should tell Banan, show him what she wanted, but to her joy he didn't need to be asked. He slid a hand down, using his thumb on her bud and, at the same time and with the same rhythm, moving his cock in and out of her wet avenue.

'Oh, yes ... please!' she cried. 'Do it just like that!'

He chuckled and lowered his head, suckling at her breast and her clit swelled and throbbed, echoing the sensation, and she could feel the orgasm mounting within her until it exploded in a welter of pleasure. 'You came for me,' he exclaimed jubilantly, and abandoned himself, pursuing his own apogee.

She felt his cock swell inside her as he pumped hard, felt the surge of warm spunk fired into the condom. He spurted, once, twice, thrice, then collapsed across her and her arms went round him, holding him tightly.

Drowsily she watched the play of light moving across the beamed ceiling, and listened to the birds singing and the noisy gulls shrieking overhead, and the soft, swish-swish of the sea as it ran up the beach. This was peace. She was relaxed, as a woman has the right to be after a thorough shafting. Banan's breathing became even, and she closed her eyes and took a nap. There was time aplenty to finish the painting.

***

Caitlin was taking a break from both posing and the hotel. Belle seemed perfectly content to shoulder the responsibility while Caitlin explored the area, posed for Banan, signed cheques and was generally around to put the guests at their ease. They liked the idea that she was Miss Macey's great-niece. It formed a continuity that the regulars found comforting, whilst those booking in for the first time, were pleased to find such a good-looking and pleasant young woman in charge, although, of course, the inestimable Belle was always on hand.

I'm taking advantage of her good nature, Caitlin thought guiltily every time she escaped to the studio to be painted and fucked. She simply couldn't resist Banan, with his Irish charm and awesome talent, sure that he was destined to become a great name in the art world.

'Don't go into one, but I really like him a lot,' she admitted to Saskia during one of their telephone conversations.

'Caitlin, don't go there,' Saskia groaned. 'You have the hots for him, but you've had so few lovers to compare him with. You know so little about men. Don't be walked over. He's manipulating you and, from what you've said about her, Mrs Godwin is possessed of managerial brio and only too willing to keep her position by having you banging away with him when you should be paying attention to your hotel.'

'I wish you were here,' Caitlin said earnestly. 'I suppose you're right. You know so much more about people than me. I'm a pushover, and take them at their word. I can't believe Banan's insincere.'

'Get a life, babe.' Saskia sounded impatient.

'He probably enjoys bonking you. What bloke wouldn't? But he obviously wants to keep on the right side of you. You're the boss. You could turn him out of his snug little retreat and he'd have nothing. Same with Mrs Godwin. She doesn't want to move, does she? Perhaps she hopes you'll make her a partner.'

'So I might,' Caitlin returned defensively. 'I don't think I could cope with it alone. As for Banan . . . ?'

'Artists are usually one hundred per cent selfish. They have to be. It's the nature of the beast. Genius has to be protected, pampered, fostered and it doesn't much matter who foots the bill. I'm just warning you to be aware of this, that's all. Don't fall for him headlong. Try a couple of other cocks up your punani first.'

After cogitating on this advice, Caitlin decided to give posing a miss for the morning and drove down to the quayside. Somewhere in the back of her mind floated the notion of buying a bikini and a sexy pair of shorts. She was only very gradually beginning to grasp the fact that she had money in her bank account, rather a lot of money. There was no longer any need to save for a rainy day. It looked as if the weather would stay fine over High Tides for ever.

There were several trawlers and a couple of yachts at anchor in the harbour. She thought of Mr Griffen and wondered if he would sail round the coastline and moor there. He had seemed more than enthusiastic when she reported into his office during her last stay in Granchester. The car park was already full of holidaymakers, some off-loading from a tourist coach. Though nowhere near as big as

Newquay, Queensbury had its own particular attractions, not the least of which being the Standing Stones, the bewitched Dancing Princesses. A money prize had been offered to the person able to count them three times and come up with the same number.

Caitlin could feel the rays scorching her bare shoulders and arms and was glad she had taken the precaution of using sun lotion. Her top was low necked, held up by two slender straps. She wished it were strapless, disliking white marks spoiling her tan. She had got used to lying naked outside Banan's cottage, basking there with him in the noonday heat, embracing him as if they were a pagan nymph and shepherd, the sun like a golden bowl between the trees, pouring forth its libation. Just as he poured his into me, she thought and was aware that her panty gusset was sticky.

I don't want to give him up, she thought rebelliously. Saskia seems to think that her unflattering opinion of men is carved in stone. I'm sure she's wrong.

She wandered along, looking at the shops. They were mostly built of local materials and had probably once been cottages for fishermen and their families. Now they catered for the summer influx, gift-shops, cafés and pubs. Caitlin stopped outside the largest of these, the Lobster Pot. It had bay windows of dimpled glass, and a double door in the centre. On the pavement outside were goods that would appeal to the boating enthusiast. Coils of rope of varying thickness, tubs of brass fittings, fishing rods and lines, shrimping nets, waterproof sou'westers, peaked caps, neoprene wet-suits, every gadget imaginable. Just inside the door, behind a basket of beach balls, was a cardboard box of red, blue and green rubber flip-flops of all sizes, and a rack of beachwear.

Caitlin entered. She wasn't the only customer and a woman with a mass of frizzy, peroxide hair was serving behind the old-fashioned mahogany counter. She was thin and sharp-featured, wearing a crop-top and a skirt far too short for her years. She looked harassed. Caitlin did a double take when a man appeared from somewhere at the back. He was big, not exactly tall but chunky, chestnut-haired and bearded and ruggedly handsome, his magnificent physique shown off by a pair of blue jeans and a plain black T-shirt.

He looked across and saw Caitlin watching him. He smiled. She blushed and thumbed through the swimwear, finding and holding out a bikini that consisted of three tiny fake leopard-skin triangles designed to cover the nipples and pubic slit and not much else. The price tag read, £49.99. Saskia wouldn't have hesitated.

'It's a new range,' said a deeply masculine voice beside her and she turned to see the shopkeeper. 'Of course, it's not for everyone. You have to have the figure for it.' His tone suggested that she had, and he added, 'I'm Jon Trent, by the way, and I own all this.'

'There's not much of it for that amount of money,' she said tersely, embarrassed by the costume and wishing the floor would open and swallow her up.

'That's how it goes with designer swimwear . . . less is more, if you get my drift.'

'OK. I'm looking for shorts, too,' she managed to get out. He pointed to another rail and left her to it.

She was spoilt for choice. Racy little numbers were definitely in. She picked out a couple, one in stonewashed denim, the other in white linen. Both were almost indecently brief, low slung so that a navel ring and the top of one's bum crease could be flaunted.

'Would you care to try them on? And the bikini?' asked Jon, and she wished he wasn't so overpoweringly macho, wished he hadn't brought them closer by telling her his name. That Cornish burr, those amber eyes and gypsyish, curling hair, that deep, all-year-round tan. What was he doing serving in a chandlery? He should be braving the high seas, hauling at the nets and dredging up shoals of fish.

'Ah . . . yes. I guess I'd better . . . for size, you know,' she stammered and followed where he led.

She heard him say to the assistant, 'Have your lunchbreak now, Hilary. I'll take over.'

The shop was emptying and, after Hilary had gone, Jon turned the notice on the door from OPEN to CLOSED. Caitlin eyed him nervously, then slipped into the changing room and, drawing the curtains tightly, put down her bag and started to undress. The long mirror reflected her image as she popped on the bikini thong and adjusted the ties each side. It was incredibly brief and wisps of fair hair protruded on either side of the crotch; she would have to shave or use a depilatory cream. She was taken unaware by the spasm of lust that stirred her pussy as she looked at herself in that revealing tanga.

The two scraps of material slung on a neck-cord with further ties at the back were hardly adequate to cover, let alone support, her breasts, but they make her look divine, hoisting her nipples and giving her a stunning cleavage. She strutted about the cubicle, wishing she were wearing the highest of high-heeled sandals.

She froze, instinct telling her she was being observed. 'Who's there?' she cried shrilly and grabbed for her clothes.

'It's me. Jon. Can I come in?' He didn't wait for permission, opening the curtains and standing there.

'Really, this isn't on,' she protested, but nevertheless wanted to display herself to him in that tiny leopard-print outfit.

'I wondered if you needed any help,' he said, with a disarming smile. 'I must say, you look wonderful. It really suits you.'

'Thank you. I'll take it. Now would you please leave me alone to try on the shorts.'

He didn't leave, simply stepped closer, and, before she could stop him, he had taken her breasts in his large hands, his thumbs revolving over the hard nipples. 'Do you really want me to go?' he whispered.

She wanted to say yes, but her knees had weakened so much that she clung to his shoulders for support. He took this for acquiescence, moved one of his hands and slid his fingers round her neck until his palm cupped the base of her skull. He drew her towards him and his mouth took possession of her lips, his beard soft and silky. Stunned, she stood stock still, reaching up on tiptoe, her arms straight at her sides as she felt the press of his tongue insistently exploring her. It was a totally unexpected situation, and she hadn't been prepared for the speed of it or the desire flaming

85

through her. Her nipples crimped and her belly pressed into the hot hardness of his cock coming erect beneath his jeans.

This couldn't be happening to her, could it? It was the kind of scenario Saskia would orchestrate. He was a stranger, therefore would be doing this through pure lust, not with any ulterior motive. And as for her? She was shucking off her old ideals. It was better to experiment, as Saskia had advised, take many men into her punani, learning all the way.

Jon unfastened the cords that held the bikini bottom together, and whipped it away from between her legs. His fingers probed her dampness, curling round the floss and parting the wings, dipping into her vulva and then palpating her clit. She squirmed, and he ground his thumb against her in a knowing way, using just the right pressure. She threw back her head, her mouth open on a silent cry as he brought her to the peak.

'That was good, yes?' he murmured, his voice thrilling down her spine. 'Now we try it this way.'

He leaned against the wall, opened his flies and took out a penis that was large, solid and perfectly formed, though lacking its foreskin. The head was red and angry-looking, dew seeping from the slit, and he handled it as if well used to masturbation, rubbing the loose skin of the stem up and down, then circling the glans with his fingers before rolling on a silvery rubber.

Then, wrinkling his jeans round his knees, Jon reached for her, lifted her effortlessly, parted her legs and impaled her on his cock. She cried out as he penetrated further, inch by inch, until he was buried to the hilt inside her, lifting her up and down on that impressive tool. She clung to him, arms round his neck, the echoes of her climax satisfied by riding him. She wrapped her legs round his waist and rocked her hips, wanting to feel the vitality that would surge through him as he came. Suddenly, she yearned to know man after man – their bodies, their desires, their cocks. Big ones, small ones, fat and thin ones – as many as she could manage. She wanted them filling every orifice, and practising perversions on her: binding her, whipping her, blindfolding her. These thoughts were new and strange, then she realised that they had been buried in her subconscious for years. It had taken her recent experiences to set them free.

Jon was in control, and she allowed him to raise and lower her as if she were a lifeless doll, only there for his pleasure. She was carried along on the crest of his passion, and he pumped harder, his thigh muscles quivering as he held her under the buttocks and thrust even deeper. She grunted like an animal as he rammed into her, his frenzied movements gaining momentum until he shouted loudly, his face like that of a tortured saint as he let go in her depths.

He grew still, then gently eased his cock from her and set her down on her feet. He removed the condom from his limp prick, then caressed her and said, 'Take the shorts home and try them on, if you want. Are you a visitor, or a resident?'

'I live here, at High Tides,' she said, coming to herself slowly, feeling utterly dazed. 'I'm Caitlin Colbert.' She didn't add any more of her history and her name seemed to mean nothing to him. Obviously he hadn't heard of her arrival in

Queensbury, and this added to that special feeling she was developing for him.

She took off the bikini top, and he helped to clip her bra at the back, then she pulled up her panties and skirt. 'How much do I owe you?' she asked, brisk and businesslike when they went back to the shop and he turned the door notice around.

'Don't worry about it,' he began, but she would have none of this.

'I'd rather pay,' she said, hardly able to believe what she had just done with him. She didn't know whether to be glad or sorry, only that Saskia would have approved.

'If you're sure. Should the shorts not fit, then return them,' he answered, his face perfectly straight but a twinkle in his eyes. 'Perhaps we can meet again soon. Would you like to come out in my boat? She's called the *Ariadne* and is moored just over there. My father was a fisherman and his father before him, but the industry is not what it was. I bought this shop instead of carrying on the trade, but I take sightseers round the bay sometimes, just to keep my hand in and give the old girl an airing.'

'I'd like that, Jon,' she said, a little shy about using his name. 'Maybe we could sail over to that island out there.'

He looked dubious and shook his head. 'Bard's Peak? I think not. It's out of bounds. Not only is it a bird sanctuary, but it belongs to Tristan Trevellyan, and he doesn't take kindly to trespassers.'

CHAPTER

5

That name cropping up again. Who was Tristan and why did everyone seem to be so in awe of him?

Caitlin mentioned it to Belle.

'Tristan Trevellyan? Can't say I know much about him,' she answered, as they enjoyed a drink on the terrace in the cool of the evening. 'He's too potent for my blood.'

Caitlin was getting a taste for cocktails with amusing names and little paper umbrellas with sticks poking through plump green olives or glacé cherries. They had been invented by the Bright Young Things during the Roaring Twenties in the aftermath of World War One, so Belle said. The pool gleamed invitingly and Caitlin was wearing her new bikini under her cotton sundress. She had trimmed her pubes before putting it on, a process that drew attention to her clit and made her horny.

The shorts had fitted just fine; all she needed was the bottle to wear them. She had said nothing to anyone about Jon, reserving her confession till she rang Saskia. As for Banan? She decided to keep shtoom. For all she knew he might be shagging half a dozen other women, so what did it matter if she spread it around, too?

'So, tell me what you do know. Have you met him? Has he been here?' Caitlin unbuttoned her dress and slipped it off. Her skin had darkened to a coppery tone, gleaming like satin from an application of after-sun lotion.

'Fancy him, do you?' Belle asked, eyes screened by her dark glasses. She wore a sleek purple swimsuit, cut high at the sides and low at the neck and back, and was nearly as tanned as Caitlin.

'No,' she lied, refusing to admit that her feelings for him were ones of lust. She hadn't even met the man!

'Then you'll be the only female in the neighbourhood who doesn't cream her knickers at the mere mention of him,' stated the forthright Belle. 'He's too arrogant for me, but even the wild rumours that he's a psycho don't put them off. If anything it adds to his allure.'

'Really?' Caitlin said coolly and lowered herself into the pool via the curved marble steps at the shallow end.

The water crept up her legs and thighs and round her fork, entering her cleft and kissing her anal ring. Her belly felt the touch of those tickly ripples, and she sank down till she was breast high, then struck out, swimming strongly to the deepest part. There she rested, holding on to the conduit where the water was constantly filtered and then returned.

Belle sat on the edge close to her. 'Tristan has been to High Tides, but not for ages . . . not since his wife left.'

'You think she walked out on him, or that he murdered her?' Caitlin kicked her legs beneath the surface, admiring their dark sheen accentuated by the blue ceramic tiles. Soon submerged lights would come on automatically.

'I don't honestly know.' With a muted splash, Belle slipped in beside her; she was a shapely woman, very supple for her age, and Caitlin had the urge to touch her, but restrained herself, rather alarmed, as she had been when she found that she fancied Saskia.

'He's not taken up with anyone else,' Belle went on. 'Shuns people and society. Lives at Lyons Court alone, except for a couple of maids and his manservant, a creepy bloke called Robert Vintner. Now him I don't like. He gives me the willies. I see him occasionally doing the shopping. He's only a bloody housekeeper but ponces about as if he owns every stick and stone in Queensbury, just like his employer. They have daily cleaners in, but they don't last long because of super fussy Robert. It wasn't like that when Portia Trevellyan was around. Everyone got on with her.'

'Tristan must have loved her very much.'

'It seems that way, but don't get any ideas of offering solace. Stay away from him, Caitlin. Haven't you got enough on your plate with Banan?'

'That I have,' Caitlin replied, swimming off again and thinking: if only you knew about Jon Trent. And she suddenly wished he was there, wearing nothing at all, and she tried to guess what he would look like.

Caitlin shivered as she looked up at the towering cliffs that sloped down towards dense woods on the far side of the cove. Against all advice, she had rounded the jutting rocks from which Tristan had appeared on his stallion. Now she was on his private property, a horseshoe-shaped bay, and was about to brave Bluebeard in his castle. The sea was far out. She had several hours before she'd have to retreat and return to the beach below High Tides.

Banan had gone to St Ives on business and Jon was, presumably, doing a brisk trade in the Lobster Pot. Caitlin had spent the morning checking in a fresh consignment of laundry and, after lunch, had given in to the urge to investigate her renowned and mysterious neighbour. She wore a sleeveless top and an old pair of shorts, having toyed with the new ones and then decided against them. But she had been unable to resist putting on the leopard bikini under her sensible attire. Supposing – *just supposing* – she met Tristan and they hit it off. Not that she intended anything of the kind, but wouldn't she feel more confident if she was sporting something flashy?

'You're a fool,' Saskia's phantom voice snapped in her brain. Caitlin had phoned her last night and told her about Jon.

She had approved, saying, 'That's my girl. Play the field. Why d'you want to meet this upper-crust dude ... Tristan Whatshisname? Go easy. Can't it wait till I come down, then there'll be two of us?'

But no; the more Saskia argued against it, the more determined Caitlin had become to take the bull by the horns. She had slept fitfully, her head full of dreams in which she was lost in dark forests, pursued by grotesque shapes. There were hands all over her, pulling her into the undergrowth, exploring her most secret places, making her wet and desirous. She woke with a muzzy head, but after two aspirins washed down with coffee had determined to stick to her plan.

The cove was utterly deserted and curlews gave vent to mournful cries as they circled against the cloudless sky, adding to her sense of isolation. Goose-bumps lifted the fine down on her limbs. She walked across the firm sand, heading for the dunes that merged into the woods. She scaled the slippery hillocks on bare feet, the sun hot on her back, then paused, opened her pack and pulled out a bottle of mineral water, taking a long swig. By now, she had removed her top, the bikini triangles just about covering her breasts. Coarse grass pricked her feet and she put on her sensible, Velcro-fastening sandals, then moved on, welcoming the shade as she stepped into the cool, shadowy, pine-scented gloom.

A track wound upwards and she guessed this was the one Tristan would take when riding. Did it eventually lead to Lyons Court? She was burning with curiosity, and something else that she refused to recognise as a mixture of dread, excitement and spine-tingling desire. It was utterly silent; no bird-calls or breeze ruffling the trees, just an oppressive quiet that made her think of horror films. What a place to bury a corpse! So many dells, tangled root complexes and rabbit holes in the forest floor, part-covered in pine needles. Had the police set their team of experts searching there for Portia?

This was a grisly thought and, nerves taut as bowstrings, she jumped violently when a branch cracked behind her and a voice said, 'Don't you know you are trespassing, Miss Colbert?'

Almost wetting herself with fright, she spun round. Tristan was right behind her, a stern expression on his saturnine face. 'I'm sorry,' she spluttered, holding her bag in front of her like a shield. 'I didn't think you would mind me exploring further than the cove next door. How do you know who I am?'

'Word travels fast,' he answered seriously, and looked at her with mockery, anger and something indefinable that made her pussy clench and her clit stir. 'But that doesn't give you leave to pry. This is very private land, Miss Colbert, and I like it that way.'

I knew he'd be tall, she was thinking, even as she sought a valid excuse for being there, but I didn't quite realised just *how* tall. He must be six foot five. The top of my head doesn't reach the pit of his throat. And his hair is so long and black, and his face would be too perfect were it not for the strong jaw with the cleft in the centre and that pronounced nose.

'I'm a newcomer here,' she faltered, groping for a tree trunk and leaning against it gratefully, her knees wobbling.

'Privacy is privacy all the world over.' His voice was low and controlled and she yearned to break him, to have him gasping with passion, and was shocked at herself for even contemplating such a thing. 'There's a Keep Out sign on the beach. I assume you can read, Miss Colbert.'

This riled her, and she turned away. 'I can, Mr Trevellyan, but I didn't notice it. If you'll excuse me, I'll go back the way I came and trouble you no more. Goodbye.'

'Wait,' he commanded so forcefully that she stopped. 'What was it you wanted to see? The woods? The house? Myself? I know I'm something of a bogeyman round here. I expect someone has told you about my wife.'

'Not much,' she said, quite frightened now. He looked so grim and his hands were clenched into white-knuckled balls. 'I've not been here long. No time to catch up on local history, though I'd like to . . . not about you, of course. I didn't mean that, but stories about Queensbury's past . . . smugglers and wreckers and all that,' she ended lamely.

He looked at her suspiciously, the dark bar of his brows drawn into a frown. His stormy eyes swept down over her. She was extremely conscious of the tiny cups that held her breasts and wanted to dive for the top that she'd stuffed into her bag. What must he think of her, part Girl Guide, part Ibiza vamp?

'You like history?' he asked slowly.

'It was one of my subjects at university, along with English,' she returned, thinking: now he can't dismiss me as a brain-dead bimbo. 'I've graduated and was going to be a teacher, until the news came through that I had inherited High Tides.'

'It happened just like that? Out of the blue?'

'Yes,' she said, steadier now, no longer imagining him attacking her and hiding her body. 'I'd almost forgotten I had a Great-Aunt Mary, though we used to visit her when I was tiny. She and my mother quarrelled, you see, and she left nothing to her and everything to me. I wasn't sure what to do at first, but once I'd come down here again and seen how fantastic it was, I just had to stay.'

'It is a fabulous spot. One may try to leave but one always returns. At least, most people do.' He added this last statement quietly, as if to himself, and Caitlin knew that he referred to his wife. He straightened and returned to the present. 'Perhaps you would like to continue exploring. I'll be your guide,' he offered.

Caitlin was astonished and still wary, but as he led her along the bridle path she dared to ask, 'Where is your horse today?'

'Merlin's at stud, covering a mare at a friend's stable.'

She had a quick flash of Tristan astride the stallion, but today there were no jodhpurs and he wore instead a pair of black canvas trousers with a wide belt adorned with a silver buckle and a black polo sweater. No riding boots, but casual slip-ons worn without socks.

What did he intend towards her? He walked a little ahead, stopping now and again to help her over a tricky bit of terrain, and every time this happened her stomach fluttered as if invaded by dozens of butterflies. His hand was warm, dry palmed and confident. She wanted him to touch her more and more, even faking a stumble so that he reached out and steadied her. As she swayed into him at one point, she inhaled a whiff of heady perfume that was wholly his. It was a blend of expensive aftershave and body spray, the rich odour of his thick hair, and another smell, too, musky and masculine – that of recently showered genitals.

They came out into a buttercup-starred meadow where coffee-coloured cows with swinging udders browsed on the lush verdure. 'Your herd?' she asked, creeping a little closer to him as the doe-eyed creatures lifted their horned heads and watched them pass.

'Yes,' he replied, with a slow smile. 'Are you

afraid of them?'

'I'm a city girl. Not used to livestock. The country is rather alarming.'

'That's what Portia used to say,' he muttered, and it was as if he were speaking to himself.

They crossed the meadow and passed through a gate that led into parkland. The trees thinned and there, looking like a doll's house in the distance, stood the high walls and rooftops of Lyons Court. Parts were still monastic, the rest mostly Tudor with touches of Palladian, a haphazard mixture of architectural styles affected at the whims of its lords down the ages.

'My home,' Tristan announced, with more than a hint of pride.

'What a place!' she whispered, even more impressed by its size as they drew closer.

He led her round to the back, avoiding the front door that was reached by shallow granite steps. It looked as high as the entrance to a church. They passed the stable block and garaging for several cars and crossed a cobbled yard to where a door stood open. A man sat sunning himself on a wooden bench outside. He wore a white shirt with the sleeves rolled above his elbows, a striped waistcoat and well-cut trousers. He jumped up when he saw them.

'Robert, bring tea and cakes to the library,' Tristan said.

'Yes, sir. At once, sir,' the man said, flicking her a glance, and beneath his almost obsequious manner there lay a thread of insolence. Caitlin registered his name. So this was the Robert who Belle had spoken of so disparagingly.

He was spare of frame, with small hands and

feet. His clothing was neat to the point of obsession, his jaw clean-shaven and his sandy hair slicked back. He was good-looking in a bland way, but Caitlin was aware of something odd behind his obliging expression and over-friendly eyes.

'I wouldn't trust him further than I could throw him,' Belle had said, and Caitlin could now see what she meant.

Of course, he fitted into his surroundings perfectly, the archetypal gentleman's gentleman. 'Robert's been with me for years,' Tristan said as he took her from the kitchen by way of a green baize door, and up some stairs to the Great Hall.

The ceiling was beamed, the floorboards old and wide and made of polished oak. There were portraits of Trevellyan forebears, and mounted heads of deer with spreading antlers, and bears and tigers, too. A huge stone fireplace stood empty in the centre of one wall, embellished with mythological figures and cornucopia. If Caitlin had occupied its wide hearth she would have been dwarfed. The space between the andirons was big enough to hold logs the size of a man.

'It must be wonderful at Christmas,' she breathed, enraptured. 'A blazing fire and a tall fir tree with lights and decorations, and ivy wreaths and holly.'

His expression darkened and, 'I don't usually bother with that kind of nonsense,' he said.

'But surely . . . you must have had parties here. It's built for it.'

'Once I did, but I haven't bothered since I've been alone.'

'Don't feel sorry for him,' hissed Saskia's ghost in her ear. 'Don't start imagining cosy nights by the fire.

It's all a load of crap! The first Mrs T is probably rotting in the cellar somewhere.'

The library surpassed Caitlin's wildest dreams. Those at university had been nothing like so splendid. It carried that special odour of must and dust, old parchment and printers' ink. The walls were lined with glass-fronted shelves behind which nestled leather-bound tomes and first editions, manuscripts and sheaves of sketches, probably left there after jolly weekends by distinguished literary figures or exponents of the brush.

Deep chairs, rich Persian rugs scattered across the floor like bright islands on a burnt-umber sea, a desk, another grandiose fireplace, and a seat built into the window embrasure that curved round the huge bay with its diamond panes and leaded lights ornamented with armorial bearings in stained glass. These crests, more than anything, brought home to her how important the Trevellyans had once been – knights, barons and men of power. And their descendent was standing beside her, his eyes exploring her curves, an ironic smile lifting his sensual, beautiful mouth.

She was shockingly aware of the informality of her dress. 'Could you point me in the direction of the ladies room?' she asked, her face flaming. 'I feel out of place like this and would like to put on my T-shirt. I wasn't expecting an invitation to tea in a palace.'

'My dear girl, this is not exceptional,' he said, and his smile lit up the whole of his face, transforming it, banishing that formidable sternness and making him look almost boyish 'You should visit some of the other manors in Cornwall and Devon if you want to see buildings approaching palatial.' Then he sobered, and his eyes skimmed her bare shoulders, her back and breasts so shamelessly revealed by the halterneck. 'Don't cover up,' he said huskily. 'You are quite the loveliest thing I've seen in ages. It gives me great pleasure just to look at you. Will you tell me how old you are?'

'Twenty-three,' she replied.

'You seem untouched and sincere,' he continued. 'Can it be that there are still decent, truthful girls around?'

She didn't know where to look, her conscience troubling her when she thought about Banan and Jon. She hoped Tristan wouldn't find out she had shagged them.

'I was taught that it was a sin to lie. My mother used to tell me that I'd get pimples on my tongue if I did,' she said, only too aware that his nearness was making her nipples hard, two sharp points lifting the feline-dappled cups.

'Can I believe you?' he murmured, his hands hovering as if he was about to take her breasts in their warm palms, fondle and caress them, and she imagined him burying his face between them, kissing the hot flesh.

Just then Robert came in carrying a silver salver. Caitlin sat on a small, gilded chair in front of a low buhl table and Robert set the tray down and poured. The scent of Assam spiced the air. This was *real* tea, not brewed from sweepings enclosed in supermarket sachets.

'Milk and sugar, Miss Colbert?' Robert asked deferentially, and she wondered how he knew her name.

'Milk, no sugar,' she answered.

He withdrew and Tristan proffered the cakes. Caitlin was too nervous to eat, but took one out of politeness. They drank their tea in silence, and then he said, 'Next time you come, I'll take you on a guided tour.'

There was to be a next time, then? Caitlin swallowed a scalding mouthful and, gaining courage, asked, 'Would it be possible to see Banan's portrait?'

'Of Portia?' He looked so bleak that she cursed herself for raising the subject.

'Please. He's told me about it. I'm posing for him at the moment and the subject came up.'

'You're posing for Banan? In the nude?'

'Yes,' she said tersely, angered by the question. It had nothing to do with him who she posed for, naked or not.

'But you hardly know him, do you?' He was lecturing her as if she were a recalcitrant child, and she stiffened her spine, her chin lifting mulishly.

'As a matter of fact, he was the first person I met when I arrived from Granchester,' she said icily. 'He had been sent to collect me, and was most kind.'

A subtle change had come over Tristan. No longer an affable host, he had become tyrannical once again. 'Oh, well, if you want to cheapen yourself, it's up to you,' he snarled.

'I'm not cheapening myself. He's a considerable artist. You must have thought so too, if you commissioned him to paint your wife,' she retorted.

They had both risen to their feet, and he was standing near her, his arm brushing her shoulder, staring into her eyes as if he would wrest secrets from her soul. However the proof of his arousal was damning, thrilling her with the sight of that long bough swelling against his thigh. Suddenly, she was filled with raging desire and a desperate hunger to know this man, in every way. She was aware, too, that if she let him into her mind, then there would be no turning back. It was a terrifying thought.

She was unable to move, facing him with tingling nipples and an ache in her cunt, but he didn't try to touch her. She longed to press her body against his.

It was Tristan who broke the spell. 'Come with me,' he said, and led her back into the hall and up the wide, sweeping staircase. He paused at the first landing and she found herself face to face with a life-sized portrait. The beauty of the subject took her breath away.

Banan had said that Portia had been beautiful, but Caitlin had not been prepared for the sheer glory of the woman. The portrait had been executed in a more realistic style than Banan's current work. It was robust, whereas now his ladies were wraithlike. Portia's face was as lovely as an angel's, yet showed signs of hedonistic living, with worldly, sherry-coloured eyes and scarlet lips curved in a provocative smile. She had tousled auburn hair, a mane of curls that tumbled over her shoulders and halfway down her back. It matched the foxy thatch covering her plump mound.

The pose was arresting, the perfectly formed naked body lying on a couch spread with a vivid throw, the delicate flesh shimmering in contrast. The breasts were full and firm, with nipples the size and colour of cobnuts, and the whole was a stunning portrait of a woman in her prime, confident, determined and a law unto herself.

'One of Banan's best,' Tristan observed, gazing up at it with an expression Caitlin couldn't fathom.

She was feeling so dishevelled, a scruffy urchin in shorts and bikini bra, hot, sweaty and oozing sex juice. Portia would never have appeared like that, not if she were pursuing a man. And am I in pursuit of Tristan? Caitlin asked herself.

'She's gorgeous,' she managed to croak, bitterly jealous of this woman who she saw as a rival.

'She was indeed,' Tristan said, never taking his eyes from the picture. 'And probably still is, wherever she's gone. There'll never be anyone like her.'

'I'd better be going,' Caitlin said, afraid of betraying her disappointment. It was obvious that he still loved his missing wife.

'I didn't do away with her, you know,' he said abruptly.

'I never thought you did. Well, not seriously and certainly not since we've met.'

'Oh, Caitlin! You're so different to her,' he said suddenly, and spanned her buttocks with one hand, pulling her towards him. She felt the tumescence behind his trousers. It pressed into her belly.

He held her firmly and lowered his face to hers, capturing her lips, his tongue penetrating boldly. Her head fell back against his arm and she surrendered to her pent-up feelings. His mouth was all consuming, such passion, as if he hadn't had a woman for a long time.

Then from below, a door opened and closed and voices could be heard. Tristan released her, looking almost as bewildered as she felt as he said, 'I'll take you home by road. The tide will be on the turn now and it can be dangerous on the beach if you don't know your way around.'

'All right,' she muttered, hoisting up her bag, careful not to look at the painting again. It was too unnerving.

'Would you like to come over for dinner one

103

evening?' he asked after the short car journey that had been accomplished in silence.

Caitlin opened the Bentley's passenger door and got out. He had braked at the entrance to High Tides' gravelled drive. 'Thank you. I'd like that,' she said.

'I'll ring you,' he promised, and drove off.

It was late afternoon and the hotel had sunk into the somnolence and inertia of a hot summer's day. She could hear some of the guests splashing around in the pool and would have liked a dip herself, but preferred to swim alone. As she passed Belle's room, she caught the sound of subdued male laughter and the manageress's throaty chuckle. Barry's with her, she thought, and the heat that Tristan had aroused in her pussy threatened to engulf her.

She hurried, entered her suite, closed the door behind her and headed for her bedroom. She felt shaken and confused, not knowing what to think of the recent encounter with the local laird. The hot waves of lust that had swept her when he kissed her lingered on. She sank into a chair in front of the dressing table and opened her legs wide, then inserted a hand into the elasticated waistband of her shorts and the front of her bikini thong and let her fingers cruise over her belly and tangle with her waxed pubic bush. The feel of it was novel and arousing, so crisp in the centre and smoothly bare at the edges.

Her clitoris was throbbing and she wetted her finger in her juices and spread it over the little bud, rubbing it purposefully. Her left hand found her breasts and undid the halter, baring them, luscious and hard with want. Her reflection in the mirror aroused her even more. It showed the image of a wanton slut pleasuring herself. She got to her feet and stripped, then resumed her pose, a voyeur intent on observing as her hand spread wide her labial lips and her finger massaged the wet and shiny organ between them. She would have liked to delay, heaping fire on fire, then holding off, teasing her nubbin, but her need was too urgent and she frigged herself fiercely, thinking of Tristan and bringing about a thunderous climax.

Tristan had been disturbed by his meeting with Caitlin. This made him angry. He didn't like the calm of his existence ruffled, having fought so hard and so long to be unaffected by emotion. This had always been so, as far back as he could remember.

An only child, he had never been close to his parents, the heir they had wanted to carry on the line, but not a longed-for baby. He had been handed over to a nanny, then packed off to prep school at five. His mother died, and he felt no grief. His father remained a remote figure, and there was little contact with him during vacations from the prestigious public school where Tristan was a boarder. He spent most of his time alone, looked after by the housekeeper and head butler. But it wasn't possible to make friends with them; they were beneath him.

A senior member of Government, his father was rarely at Lyons Court and Tristan was unaffected when, while an undergraduate at Oxford, he was informed that his father had died and he was now responsible for the Trevellyan fortune. He had attended the funeral, left the estate in the hands of a manager, finished his course, and then retired to

Cornwall. There he had remained, a quiet, studious young man, until the fatal day when he had been introduced to Portia.

She had turned his life upside down. Whereas once Lyons Court had slumbered, she woke it into turbulent life. There had been parties and galas and fêtes, and their wedding had been the event of the year. She had all the attributes required for a Trevellyan bride – the right connections, social standing and a large amount of blue blood in her veins. Added to this were sexual allure, a vivacious personality and a ravishing face and figure.

Tristan had thought himself the luckiest man alive.

Now he walked up the grand staircase slowly and stood before her portrait. He looked at his wife and thought about Caitlin. She was nothing like the flamboyant creature he had married – shy, reserved, pretty but unaware of her potential. When he had seen her round the headland from his lookout on the cliff-top, he had recognised her as the woman he had met on the beach with Banan. He had been impressed by her then, but disapproving of her companion; Banan was an inspired artist, but never short of willing lovers.

Robert had an ear to the grapevine and soon filled Tristan in when, on his return from their first meeting, he wanted to know more about High Tides' new owner. He had watched out for her ever since, and his vigil had borne fruit. She had dared to enter his domain, and, to his consternation, he discovered that he was bewitched, unable to think of anything but her lissom body, her unsophisticated hairstyle and that touching aura of innocence that he was sure was genuine. She had entered Lyons Court like a breath of fresh air.

He would ring her soon, and arrange to pick her up and bring her back here to dine. Excitement stirred in his groin and thickened his cock. He had been celibate since Portia, afraid to make intimate contact with a woman again. His fist had become his mistress and he had reverted to the solitary pleasures he had known before she entered his life like a fiery, glittering comet.

He used the master bedchamber, a magnificent apartment that he appreciated far more than his parents had done. His father had been a bluff, hunting–shooting–fishing type of man. He had not been able to understand his only son, nor had he tried to. The fine antiques that he had taken for granted had never been displayed to full advantage until Tristan took over. Now each room was balanced and harmonious. Robert had helped; he liked to think of himself as something of an expert, and Tristan couldn't fault him. He had made himself indispensable, arriving as part of Portia's entourage, and staying on after she had disappeared. Tristan had been grateful for that, though astute enough to realise that Robert had found himself a snug and secure position as valet and general factotum.

He had noticed the calculating way in which Robert had looked at Caitlin. Was he wondering how his own grasp on Lyons Court would be affected should his master decide to introduce a woman there – possibly even marry again? This brought a wry smile to Tristan's lips. Marry? Hardly, with his first wife still on the missing person's list.

The room was filling up with shadows, the fiery

ball of the sun sinking in a swathe of apricot, crimson and washed-out green-blue. Rooks cawed and circled beyond the window, seeking roosts for the night and bats gyrated, swarming from the ivy-hung bell tower in pursuit of winged insects. It was a scene like many another he had viewed, yet this evening it seemed different, as if everything held a special radiance as he allowed optimism to bloom where there had once been despair. It seemed incredible that this transformation had been brought about by less than two hours with Caitlin Colbert.

In his rising excitement, he dropped a hand down and clasped his penis, testing its heat and hardness. He had wanted her so much in the library, afraid to make a wrong move that would scare her off. When he had kissed her, he had hardly been able to contain his desire, her soft lips and curling, knowing tongue making him want them round the head of his cock. This was too much for his control now, and he could feel sensation humming and buzzing inside him, from his loins to his brain, rushing in force up and down his spine. He held his cock, rubbing it against the rougher inside of his trousers. It was delicious and he savoured the feel, the wetness seeping from his slit making it slide irresistibly.

He unzipped his fly and put a hand inside, cradling the full globes of his testicles, a vision of Caitlin forming in his imagination, pretending it was her small hand weighing his balls, and her little fingers running up his cock-stem and dabbling in his pre-come. With his cods in one hand, he couldn't stop himself from touching his prick, stroking it until it swelled further, aching for relief. It was getting very slippery now, juice trickling from its single eye. Up and down he worked it, his palm curved into an imitation vagina, allowing pressure on the bulging, needy flare of the helm.

He closed his eyes and thought of Caitlin giving him fellatio, lips sucking his cock, hands playing with his scrotal sac and massaging his balls. He was moving swiftly towards the point of no return. His cock was so hard that he had to pull it back from his belly, the smallest movement or touch taking him closer and closer to the edge. His balls were hardening, his glans responding to the feel of his thumb and fingers. He gave another pump and his semen seemed to boil inside him, and the first contraction started. Now it was impossible to stop. Milky-white come jetted from him and he caught it in his other hand. He came in several spurts, screwing up his face in ecstasy. God, it was wonderful.

He stood there for a second, wringing every last drop of pleasure from his cock, then finding a tissue and wiping it before tucking it away in his trousers. Soon that image of Caitlin satisfying him would be reality.

He sat on the bed and reached for the phone, echoes of his orgasm rippling through him. A starchy receptionist replied, 'High Tides. How may I help you?'

'Put me through to Miss Colbert,' Tristan said crisply, the tumult in his balls receding to be replaced by a feeling of relaxation and peace.

CHAPTER

6

'Hello?' Caitlin said nervously, picking up the phone in her bedroom.

Caitlin. It's Tristan Trevellyan.'

She almost dropped the instrument, having half expected him to honour his promise but steeling herself against disappointment if he didn't. 'Oh, hello,' she answered, her heart beating so fast that it made her breasts tingle.

'I've had a better idea than simply inviting you here for dinner,' he went on, and she was carried away by his force and fire. 'Have you ever visited Minack?'

'No,' she breathed, quivering to the sound of his voice, her nipples and clit still alert after her orgasm, the gusset of her panties sticky with love-juice.

'It's a magnificent open-air theatre, set in a hollow on the cliff edge. Only the stage itself was constructed by man, or rather woman, as it was the dream-child of Rowena Cadam who practically built it with her own hands.'

'Where is it exactly?' Caitlin was already planning how long she might be in his company and if it meant staying the night somewhere, a prospect that thrilled and terrified her at the same time.

'It's five miles from Land's End, next to Porthcurno. Easy to do in an evening. We could go early to give ourselves time to have a meal first. What do you say, Caitlin?'

'It sounds wonderful,' she murmured, her blood singing in her veins, though her sensible self insisted that this was for the best. Cinderella would be home by midnight or there about, with her knickers on and her honour intact. As Saskia would have said: 'Treat 'em mean. Keep 'em keen.'

'It *is* wonderful,' he went on. 'During the summer, performances are given of the classics against a backdrop of sea and rocks. I'll never forget going to see *The Tempest*. It was amazing, the drama heightened by such a spectacular venue. I'm sure you'll love it.'

It was on the tip of her tongue to ask him if he'd taken Portia, but he was sounding so enthusiastic and eager that she didn't want to risk breaking the tenuous link between them that was strengthening by the second.

'I've phoned and there are seats still available for *Anthony and Cleopatra*,' he continued. 'But I'll have to book at once to be sure of getting in. When are you free? The show starts at eight.'

She wanted to say any time, but was afraid of sounding too willing. 'Well, I'll have to clear it with Belle, that's Mrs Godwin, the manageress,' she

111

prevaricated. 'I'm sometimes left in charge if she wants time off.'

'Of course,' he answered solemnly. 'Your business is of prime importance.'

'Give me your number and I'll ring you back after I've spoken with her,' she said, and went to find Belle as soon as he hung up.

Belle was amenable, though there was a frosty note in her voice when she learned the identity of her escort. Caitlin cut her off short, not wishing for yet another lecture about the dangerous master of Lyons Court.

She rang him back right away, and they settled for the evening after next. After she had put the phone down, Caitlin floated round the room on cloud nine, then pulled herself up sharply. It was no use going over the top. He had only asked her to the theatre, Godammit! She resolved to see Banan in the morning, so that he could put the finishing touches to her portrait. Then, later, she might drop by the Lobster Pot. It was essential to a girl's peace of mind that she keep more than one string to her bow.

But she was restless, preferring to take a walk on the cliffs rather than join Belle at dinner and be subjected to an interrogation concerning Tristan. She needed to be alone; somehow it seemed that she was perpetually surrounded by people. She wanted time for contemplation. It was as if she stood at a crossroads with a bewildering variety of options open to her. One thing shone crystal clear: she would not leave Cornwall.

Now she stood facing the panoramic view, the wind blowing strongly, whipping back her hair and flattening her clothes against her body. Below her the waves thundered into the cove in a surge of sea and spray, and Tristan seemed a part of that wildness.

She took a different path home, going across a heath where stacks from abandoned tin mines pointed skywards like accusing fingers. It was twilight and ghostly, with only the occasional hoot of an owl breaking the lonely silence. Caitlin found herself hurrying, snagging her skirt on clumps of heather and spiky gorse, aware that she was a stranger and, as such, not yet accepted. The stone circle glimmered in the distance, reminding her that the original Cornish were pagans, while a wayside cross and a holy well spoke of a country steeped in early Christian history. Whatever it was, the magic still existed, more black or shades of grey than white, she feared. She ran most of the way back to High Tides.

Insomnia is a curse, Caitlin concluded miserably, waking after an hour, her mind alert and active, though she was physically weary. She glanced at her wristwatch. It was only one am. Ages till morning. What was she to do during this long night's journey into day?

If I was home, in my pokey little bedsit, I'd make a cup of hot chocolate, she brooded, and take it back to bed with a packet of Rich Tea biscuits and rounds of buttered toast. But this *is* my home, she realised, pulling herself up by the bootstraps. Why don't I simply wander down to the kitchen and do just that?

She got out of bed, slipped her arms into her terry towelling dressing-gown and fastened the belt. It was a warm night and so she padded into the corridor on bare feet. The hotel was sunk in sleep. Only the grandfather clock in the hall broke the silence with its sonorous tick-tock. It has done this for a hundred years or more, she thought, long before anyone here was born, and will continue to mark the passage of time when we're dead and buried.

This played on her already over-strung nerves and she regretted venturing down into the reception area. Normally bustling, it was very different at this hour, shrouded and still. The memory of Stephen King's novel *The Shining* popped into her mind. This was about a hotel haunted by its past. What secrets did High Tides hold?

She almost turned back, then lectured herself sternly, squared her shoulders and marched resolutely to the kitchens. The light was on in the main one, and she pushed open the double swing doors and stepped boldly inside. Then she froze.

Raff was seated at one of the tables, knife and fork in his brawny fists as he tucked into a meal. His overall jacket was placed over the back of his chair. She was struck again by his hefty shoulders straining against the white singlet, and those muscular, darkly furred arms. He was extremely hirsute. She could see inky fronds sprouting at his neck and spreading over his shoulders. His back would undoubtedly be hairy, too. He had discarded his chef's hat and his cropped black hair gleamed with gel, or maybe sweat. It was certainly hot in there. The restaurant had been fully booked and meals served non-stop all evening.

Their eyes met and he said, 'I always have my supper late, when everyone else has gone and I can have the place to myself. Will you join me? Is that

114

what you came down for . . . a snack?'

'No, not exactly. I couldn't sleep and was heading for the drinking chocolate.'

'Perhaps a snifter of brandy might be better,' he suggested, indicating a balloon-shaped glass.

'Perhaps,' she agreed and slid into the chair opposite him. He poured her a drink. She sipped the dry Armagnac.

There was a curious, exciting intimacy about being there with him in the middle of the night. It was the first time they had ever been alone. No Belle, no waiters flying in and out, none of the tension that revolved round serving superlative meals to critical guests. And Raff was different, too; usually impatient, grim-faced, vexed by the real or imaginary incompetence of his staff, now he was a genial giant, all smiles and admiration, genuinely glad of Caitlin's company.

'Do you remember what I said to you the day we were introduced?' he asked, his eyes shining like wet coal, the tip of his tongue wetting his full red lips as it sought out a stray morsel of succulent pheasant soused in herb sauce.

She did, of course, but denied it, staring at him levelly and saying, 'We talked of many things.'

'Ah, Miss Colbert, I'm sure you won't have forgotten how I mentioned licking cream from the secret places of your body. I still want to do it. Won't you be my dessert?'

'This is ridiculous,' she protested, but without much conviction.

For hours she had been in a state of furious arousal that even masturbation had barely alleviated. Raff's words and the growing bulge at the fork of his white twill trousers made her want to open up to him and have him penetrate her with long, firm strokes. At least he was here, solid and human, not some nebulous dream lover as Tristran might well turn out to be.

Raff chuckled, deep in his belly, hauled himself to his feet and came round to her. He took her hands, prised her fingers free from the brandy glass and put it down. When his mouth fastened on hers, it was like being engulfed. He kissed with the same focused enjoyment as when he ate. His tongue slipped between her lips and explored her inner cheeks, her gums, her teeth. He tasted of spices and game fowl.

'You taste lovely,' he said, after freeing his mouth. 'I want more.'

He undid her belt and the robe fell open. Caitlin made a grab for it but Raff seized her wrists and held her arms apart, her breasts, belly, pubic fluff and dark cleft laid bare. She tried to squirm away, murmuring, 'Please don't . . .'

'Don't go on or don't stop?' He laughed again; laughter seemed as natural to him as breathing. His eyes shone with pleasure and anticipation and, without waiting for an answer, he lifted her up and sat her on the wide metal bench. He stripped off her dressing-gown from her shoulders but let it rest on the shiny surface beneath her.

'I don't know. I mean . . . yes, I do. Stop this at once,' she stammered, resting back on her elbows, her lower body sprawled helplessly, her legs dangling. She felt very exposed and vulnerable.

'You don't really mean that,' he teased, his eyes glittering as they studied her body. 'I think you want to experience the pleasures I can give you. Isn't that so, Miss Colbert? You look so tempting in

116

that position, so wanton, so wet. I can see the juice glistening like diamonds on your minge.'

It was a dead giveaway and she knew it. Deny it though she might, her clit was throbbing, her breasts aching with need, the nipples crimped and imploring his attention. Raff would be well endowed, she was sure, and probably as much a connoisseur of cunt as he was of haute cuisine. She was dying to try him. She parted her legs a little more, her mound pushed up by the hardness of the bench beneath her hips, her slit exposed and oozing moisture. He stared down at her treasures, and she waited with rising impatience. Why didn't he frig her?

He positioned himself between her thighs and unzipped his trousers. His penis shot out like a loaded spring, poking through his flies. Caitlin took her fill of it. The stem was as swarthy as the rest of him, and garlanded with a tracery of blue veins. The helm was dome shaped, dewy and flushed, straining from its foreskin. She encircled his cock with her fingers, feeling the velvety smooth texture, responding to the heat and stiffness of this powerful weapon. Her inner muscles convulsed, eager to clench round it, but her clit wanted caressing and fondling and bringing to the boil. Only by this means could she achieve bliss.

'Wait . . . wait,' he cautioned, easing his phallus from her grip.

Cock jutting stiffly from his fly, he went to his vacated table and dabbled his fingers in salad oil, then returned to spread it over her breasts. She wanted to resist him, but the feel of those large, hard fingers coasting over her nipples threw her into a tumult of desire. She glanced down, seeing her skin shining as it did when she applied lotion and sunbathed. The memory of hot days spent thus, of dips in the pool or the sea, of all the glorious sensuality of summer added to her arousal.

He moved and every nerve and inch of skin seemed to tingle. What was he going to do now? He picked up a length of cord and said, 'Bend your legs at the knees.'

'What?' She stared up at him with wide eyes, mesmerised by his big, meaty cock swaying above her, swollen and glistening and ready.

'Up with your legs. I'm going to truss you like a succulent little duckling. Then I shall eat you,' he said.

'Don't be silly,' she chided, trying to wriggle away. 'And wipe that oil off. You'll get my robe all messy.'

'Tut tut! That will never do, will it? Damning evidence of the boss lady screwing with her chef. Forget it, Miss Colbert. Let your hair down. Enjoy everything I have on offer, including this,' and he waggled his cock at her impudently as it poked from its nest of black, wiry hair.

He leaned over and licked the dressing from her breasts, his fleshy tongue traversing her ribcage and devouring the drops that had gathered in her navel. He went lower, cutting a swathe through her bush and nuzzling between her labia, landing unerringly on her precious clitoris and starting to suck it. But before she had time to climax, he moved his body till he was between her spread thighs and, while his thumb took his tongue's place, rotating the near-to-bursting bud, his cock head pressed against her anus, seeking entrance in that place where she was still a virgin.

'Oh . . . stop! I've never done that,' she protested feebly.

'But you'd like to try it? Another time. Now I have food in mind, not sodomy.'

She lay on her back, unresisting as he arranged her limbs to his liking. Her arms were lifted above her head and her knees bent at an acute angle. He slipped a noose around each ankle and, as he had promised, trussed her like a fowl. She was shockingly aware that her buttocks were open wide and nothing was private any more. She could see her reflection in one of the highly polished steel cabinets opposite, appalled and excited by the sight of her bare, salmon-pink furrow, wet with juice, swollen with lust, and finding that she cared for nothing save having that lust satisfied.

Raff, still exposed, dropped pieces of pheasant on to her belly, garnished them with sauce and nibbled them from his human dinner plate. 'Try some?' he suggested, and popped a morsel into her mouth. The taste was divine.

Having finished the first course, he rubbed the residue of oil into her skin with all the skill of a masseur, then left her, returning with a bowl of strawberries and a jug of cream. 'Pudding,' he said, 'But first I want to see those nipples peak,' and he took ice cubes from a bucket and balanced one on each of her breasts.

Caitlin gasped, the contrast of the cold on her heat too much to endure at first, then it warmed slightly and she began to appreciate her nipples' joyous response, and the delicious rush as Raff licked them. He poured cream over them, and licked it off with his tongue, lingering, nipping and flicking till she was near to screaming with want.

Now he moved down to her cleft and she waited breathlessly in tormented anticipation. First, she felt one finger entering her slippery cunt. It was large, hard and practised. Next he added another, and then a third. Caitlin moaned as he moved them in and out, aping coition, then protested when he removed them altogether.

'Be patient,' he counselled, and she gasped again at the feel of something soft and squishy being pushed up her. The pungent scent of strawberries mingled with her own piscine odour wafted into her nostrils.

Raff added several more, till she was stuffed with a wonderful fruity filling. She felt the chilly thick wash of cream trickling down her slit and into her hole, and then he was at her entrance. Sucking strongly, he removed the berries and took them into his mouth, sighing his satisfaction. At one point, he rose and filled her own mouth with the crushed fruit, so that she felt like a baby bird being fed by its parent.

'Taste it. Try it,' he urged, his lips smeared with the red and white dessert and glistening with her own honeydew.

His hands were slippery and they slid easily over her body, discovering every fold and erogenous zone, just as he had promised. Her delta was awash and he went down to her full, pouting lips, adding extra cream to her clit. Then he rubbed it firmly and she knew that there would be no let up till she climaxed. She moaned her need and he petted the crown of her clit. Pleasure waves rose, and then broke in a tremendous orgasm. She expected him to plunge his tool into her at that moment, but he didn't.

As she lay there recovering, he untied her legs, massaged a mixture of cream and oils into her breasts and pressed them together, forming a channel into which he inserted his massive penis. It rubbed against her sternum, lubricated with traces of berries, along with the jism seeping from his twin-lobed glans. He was heavy but braced himself on his arms, while she did the work, controlling the pressure by pushing her breasts together. She watched, fascinated, as his helm appeared at the top of her cleavage, then slid back down and up again as she massaged it with her flesh.

'Go on. Faster, faster,' he urged, sweat beading his face, driven frantic by the sight of her breast-fucking him.

He came explosively, his spunk jetting out, spattering her chest, throat and face, milky strands lodging in her hair. She felt mildly disgusted, and suddenly couldn't wait to get back to her apartment and the shower. Somewhere in her memory floated the slang term 'a pearl necklace'. She hadn't fully understood it before but now her education was coming on by leaps and bounds. Too much, too soon, perhaps.

The sun was dipping down towards the horizon beyond Minack's amphitheatre, the crimson sky gradually being swallowed by indigo night clouds. Stage lights had sprung up, illuminating the Roman tragedy.

'Messy old play, worse than a telly soap,' Tristan opined during the interval, seated close to Caitlin on one of the stone benches that stretched in a half circle facing the stage. They were reminiscent of those provided for patrons at arenas used for gladiatorial games.

'I shouldn't have thought you'd be a soap addict,' she said, smiling at him, drinking in every feature of his aristocratic face.

'I'm not,' he replied hurriedly, black brows swooping down. 'But Robert is, and insists on filling me in.'

'I watch them,' she confessed, determined to be frank. 'Not all, of course, only *Emmerdale*, *Coronation Street* and *EastEnders*.'

'And what does that say about you?' he queried, studying her with his piercing eyes.

She'd thought she had been getting on with him rather well but now felt gauche and foolish, a peasant easily amused by popular entertainment. She flushed and fanned her face with her programme. 'A great deal, I expect,' she faltered, then hid behind a play of words that she hoped sounded convincingly clever. 'My tastes are eclectic. I like all sorts of music: Gershwin and Cole Porter, and South American rhythms that make me want to dance, the rumba, the salsa and the tango. I adore opera, but not all. I love Puccini's work and some of Verdi's and *Carmen*, of course, but don't rate Mozart. The romantic twentieth-century composers thrill me . . . Ravel, Debussy and Stravinsky. I'm not moved by baroque but adore the piano works of Liszt and Chopin, and enjoy modernists like Bela Bartok and Benjamin Britten.'

He pulled a solemn face and said, 'Impressive. Come and rummage through my CDs. You'll find that I share your taste in some respects. Come back with me when the show is over. We'll drink coffee and dip into our favourites. What do you say?'

What could she say but, yes, thank you, I'd love to. He was just too attractive to refuse.

Waiting for this evening to come had been tedious, setting aside the episode with Raff, her meeting with Banan the next day and a flying visit to Jon. Banan had guessed there was something brewing and she had told him about her date with Tristan, though kept Raff and Jon to herself. Banan had added the final brush strokes to the painting of her and been noncommittal about Tristan.

'Just be careful,' he had said

She had fidgeted, leaning against the broken pillar and snapping, 'That's what Belle says. Why is everyone so against him?'

'Because he's an enigma, and that doesn't suit the locals though, truth to tell, they also play their cards very close to the chest. Haven't you noticed that feudal lords are viewed askance by the serfs?'

'Can't say I've ever been in this position before. There wasn't this class warfare in Granchester,' she had answered peevishly.

'I'll bet there was but you weren't aware of it.'

'Anyhow, I'm going to Minack with him whatever you or anyone else says.'

'OK. I'll be here when you need a shoulder to cry on,' he had teased, dipping his brushes in turpentine and wiping them clean on the tail of his shirt.

She had paced round to view the picture. It was truly splendid. 'Will you sell it to me?' she asked. One of his already hung in High Tides' entrance hall.

'I want to exhibit it in London in the autumn, and the price tag will be high,' he had said, looping an arm casually round her naked neck. 'If no one puts in a bid, then maybe we can negotiate. But I thought you weren't keen on having your guests see your bare tits.'

'It doesn't look much like me . . . far too beautiful,' she had said, leaning against him, glad of his familiar warmth and smell, but glad too when he didn't try to press her into intercourse, sensitive to her introspective mood and leaving her alone.

Later on, she had stuck her head round the door to the Lobster Pot, but Jon was snowed under by customers. She had waved to him, but that was it. There had been no one to distract her, and Tristan had loomed large in her thoughts.

Now she was with him. He had picked her up in the classic Bentley that he said had belonged to his father, and they had eaten at a quaint pub with sloping floors, blackened beams, horse-brasses and a menu recommended by gourmet magazines. Then on to the play and its awesome setting that left her on an emotional high and perfectly willing to accompany him to Lyons Court.

The moon hung above them, transforming the coastal road into a silver strip. Caitlin felt inspired by what she had just experienced, and the man in the driving seat beside her epitomised the brooding atmosphere of the centuries' old tragedy. He was a part of the moonlight and their surroundings. She could almost believe that the stories about him were true, that his passion had made him a killer. In that bedazzled moment, she didn't really care.

He hadn't touched her, but whenever he spoke his voice seemed to penetrate her, just as if he had plunged his cock into her core.

The road passed close to the Dancing Princesses,

and Tristan stopped the car. The circle loomed darkly, outlined by the moon's frosty light. 'Shall we?' he said, and leaned across her, opening the passenger door.

The wind sighed and the waves crashed against the base of the cliffs. Large and eerie, the ancient ring of stones stood solidly as if rooted there since time immemorial. They dominated the plateau, and all around was the deserted moor.

With his hand cupping her elbow, Tristan led her into the circle. It was even more weird inside. She felt enclosed, surrounded and in the clutches of the monolithic structure. His arms came about her and that in itself was a tremendous shock. Then he looked up at the dead-white face of the moon that hung like a severed head in the sky and said, 'It's supposed to be lucky to stand in the circle with your true love, but unlucky if that person proves not to be the one.'

'Do you believe that? Are you superstitious, Tristan?' she whispered, enveloped in his embrace, her breasts crushed against his chest, the long finger of his cock pressing into her belly, urgent and overheated.

'I was born here, remember? So were my forefathers. One can't fail to be superstitious living so close to the earth.'

'And you thought Portia was the love of your life. You brought her here, didn't you?' she said tremulously.

'I did,' he answered sombrely. 'But it was a long while ago and I don't want to talk about her.'

His magnetism was so compelling that she cast aside all the warnings and doubts, yielding herself to his hard embrace. His mouth closed on hers and the hot blood surged through her, beating in fierce turbulence like a stormy sea. In an instant he had her pressed up against one of the stones. It was cold as a tomb, that chill working through her thin dress. He continued to kiss her with an abandon that spoke of a crying need. Was it true that he hadn't had a woman since Portia left?

He seized her wrists and held them high above her head, then left her lips and looked down at her. 'Undress for me,' he commanded.

She shuddered, not with cold but with desire, his words like fire to her. 'All right, I will, but you'll have to free me first,' she said, and the movement of her pelvis against the solid bar of his sex was proof enough that she had no intention of escaping.

He released her wrists and she dropped her shawl and slipped down the shoestring straps of her cotton dress, baring herself to the waist. Then, boldly, she reached into the front of his shirt and tweaked the puckered discs of his nipples, dragging a groan from him. She stood, legs apart, back braced against the stone as he lifted her skirt and found her tiny tanga and pushed it impatiently aside, his fingers entering her warm, soft wetness.

She sighed, and he lowered his head and suckled her breasts, a hot line of feeling shooting down to her clit.

He understood. The steady rubbing of his slippery fingers over her bud aroused her beyond control and an orgasm ripped through her loins, rushing up her spine and exploding in a firework display.

'Now I'm going to fuck you,' he growled, and unbuttoned his trousers, then placed a hand under her buttocks and lifted her, giving her no time to look at his cock, only enough to ascertain that it was very large.

He didn't guide it in; it was hard enough and strong enough to find its own way, opening her swollen cunt and thrusting in all the way. She yelled, clung to him, her arms tight around his neck, legs round his hips as he moved her up and down on his member. With supreme control he withdrew, and she heard the rustle as he fumbled with a condom, rolling it up and over his cock. After this there was no stopping him. He was in her again, pistoning into her as if she a thing of no consequence compared with the driving force of his passion. She twisted her fingers in his hair and clamped her mouth over his, uttering strange, whimpering cries. It was as if he was punishing her with his cock, maybe with another woman in mind, one who had hurt him beyond endurance.

He went faster, bending at the knees to give more power to his pelvis, then, suddenly, he tore his lips from hers, threw back his head and gave a sharp bark, his body shuddering with the throbbing urgency of his coming. Caitlin was suspended there, still penetrated, his hands cradling her buttocks, her legs gripping his waist. Then, slowly, he pulled out and let her down till she stood on the springy turf in front of the mighty stones. She remained silent as they adjusted their clothing, and she prayed that he was not already regretting his impetuosity.

The moon had moved some way along her path, the shadows flung by the Princesses altering subtly. Caitlin wanted to touch Tristan, to kiss him and hold him.

He moved, taking her hands in his. 'I'm going to

take you home to Lyons Court,' he said. 'I haven't asked a woman this for a very long time, but I want you to spend the night with me.'

Robert saw the Bentley's headlights from the windows of his flat. It was the housekeeper's apartment on the top floor, an ideal lookout point. Nothing of importance happened in and around Lyons Court without him knowing about it.

He waited until the car had been garaged, then he crept out of the door, straining his ears down the stairwell to hear Tristan moving about in the Great Hall. He heard his footsteps as he went up to the master bedchamber, and his voice and hers (Robert recognised it as that of Caitlin Colbert), followed shortly by the sweeping strains of music and the rapturous singing of a tenor and a soprano.

Robert hurried back to his room, and dialled a number on his mobile, sexual excitement stirring his cock as he waited for someone to answer. It was late, but the person in question was a night owl. There would be no difficulty in getting through. Robert experienced an intense Machiavellian thrill. He was totally unprincipled. There was nothing he enjoyed more than beavering away behind the scenes, involving himself in plots and dirty dealings. The person who answered the phone to him was his mentor; no one was so cunning, selfish and devious.

'Who was that, darling?' asked the gorgeous woman in a black leather bustier and skirt who occupied a throne-like chair, her magnificent long legs apart, showing stocking tops and suspenders. Her feet in high-heeled boots were planted firmly on the floor, her thighs placed each side of a splendidly developed young man who was kneeling at crotch level, and licking her depilated pussy.

'Robert, reporting in,' answered the blond man she had addressed. He pocketed his phone and paced towards her, intense blue eyes fixed on her shamelessly displayed pudenda. 'It seems that Tristan has been out with a girl tonight and brought her back to Lyons Court. He's taken her to his bedroom and is serenading her with the love duet from *Madame Butterfly*. Via the hi-fi, of course.'

'That could be ominous.' The woman frowned, and dug her purple talons into the young man's scalp, stopping him in his tracks. He looked up questioningly, his lips bedewed with her juices. 'Stop now, Todd,' she commanded. 'I don't want anything to spoil my orgasm. But keep your prick nice and stiff, or you'll get a taste of this,' and she swished the short whip with several knotted thongs that she held, flicking it cross his bare back, not hard but enough to make him jerk.

He was naked except for a studded leather collar with chains reaching down to link with rings in his pierced nipples, and attached to another that passed through his foreskin. Two more naked slaves stood to attention on either side of her chair; one a glossy black Afro-Caribbean and the other a smoothly tanned Caucasian, each a magnificent specimen of manhood, chosen for their physique, the size of their cocks and the fullness of their balls. Their oiled bodies gleamed in the golden glow of braziers that lit this subterranean room, furnished in blood red and black.

Racks lined the stone walls, hung with floggers and flails, canes and birches. A crosspiece loomed large and a rack with holes positioned in advantageous places; next to these was a vaulting horse from which dangled straps and handcuffs. There were other things, too – gags and blindfolds, manacles and leg irons, the ambience one of luxury and decadence, hinting at the dichotomy between pain and extreme pleasure.

The blond man leaned across and rotated his thumb over one of the woman's prominent nipples, saying in an accent that wouldn't have been out of place at Buckingham Palace, 'Don't worry, my angel. He can't marry again for at least seven years. No one else is going to get her grubby little mitts on his fortune.'

She grinned wickedly, pushing Todd's face into her hairless mound again. 'I might just turn up one day. That would upset his apple cart.'

And her partner in crime smiled down into her beautiful face and continued to toy with her rosy-brown nipples, even while he looked at Todd's lean and tasty rump. His cock swelled under his elegantly cut velvet trousers, and he imagined the boy bending over to receive it and himself pushing his lubricated member deep into the dark depths of Todd's fundament. He would want her to watch, of course, then he might well have her as the main course, Todd being merely an appetiser.

She cupped his bulge and unzipped his fly, then had him stand closer so that she could take his long smooth phallus between her lips. He wore a Prince Albert cock-ring, with the gold circle entering the uretha and coming out at the bottom of the frenulum. Tonight he had enhanced this with black onyx beads. She ran her tongue over them and made the ring slide, adding to his sensation. While Todd brought her to ecstasy, she sucked the cock and slowly, inch by inch, let it sink across her palate till she could feel the precious metal and gems nudging her throat. It was proving too much for him; he didn't want to come that way.

He pushed his hands in her hair and moved away, his cock sensitive to the change in temperature but in no way diminishing in size. She half protested, but Todd was being just too skilful. About to tumble over into orgasm, she was blind to all else. She stiffened, spasmed and moaned and lay back, replete.

Todd released her and his eyes switched to the blond man's large appendage blatantly displayed, now covered in a black latex rubber. It contrasted with the fair bush from which the cock jutted aggressively.

'I need your slave,' the man demanded.

'Take him. He's yours,' she answered languidly, smiling vaguely.

'I'm going to fuck you, Todd,' he said.

'Oh, yes . . . please,' Todd begged, rubbing his prick frantically. Then he crawled on all fours till he reached the man's feet.

'Haven't you forgotten something?' A kick aimed at the abject Todd added to the stern words.

'Master! Fuck me, master!' the young man pleaded.

The woman had recovered and now sat up, watching keenly as his penis jerked wildly in his fist. He started to come in long, milky jets and the man leaned over him and caught some in his hand, then smeared it up the amber-hued furrow of Todd's arse. He worked his fingers into the tight anal hole while Todd knelt there. He grunted as the finger penetrated deeper, and a second was added, then moaned as they were withdrawn to be replaced by the black shrouded cock-tip. The sphincter relaxed under the pressure and Todd cried out in anguish and joy as his master thrust the whole length of his tool into him. Now he held him tightly, kneeling behind him and pumping steadily, his balls tapping against Todd's thighs.

'Go on, Guy,' she shouted encouragingly. 'Give him the shafting he deserves, and let me flog him afterwards for being a dirty little fag.'

Guy Marlow reached his zenith and emptied himself of seed. 'He's all yours,' he said, losing interest now that his lust had been appeased, dropping the black john into a bin and replacing his cock in his trousers, once again suave and controlled.

Todd resumed his place by the woman's chair. She rose and clapped her hands imperiously. At once an ample-bosomed female servant appeared, wearing a short full taffeta skirt, silk stockings, stilt-heeled shoes and a velvet corset that gave her a wasp waist and pushed her breasts high over its top.

'Drinks,' the woman ordered. 'And bring them to my bedroom. You three slaves will accompany me, just in case I get horny in the night, and you, too, Guy, once you've rung Robert and told him to carry on with the good work. I don't intend that Tristan shall even begin to imagine that he can settle down into cosy domesticity.'

Guy smiled, his pale blue eyes ice-cold. 'I'll do just that. This should prove to be fun, and don't worry about a thing. Leave it to me, Portia.'

CHAPTER

7

'Expect me on Friday,' Saskia said down the phone. 'I'll drive. That's OK. I've a map and it's mostly motorway, isn't it? I've been told it's a doddle, not like the old days when it took hours and hours. I can't wait to see all these fit blokes you've been rabbiting on about. Mind you, I've got my share here. London is just bursting at the seams. At least, the West End is and who wants to live anywhere else?'

'Listen, Saskia,' Caitlin replied earnestly. 'I'm really in love this time. Tristan is all I've ever wanted in a man. I just can't understand why he's interested in someone like me, especially after being married to the fabulous Portia.'

'Who you said vanished in peculiar circumstances,' Saskia reminded, perching her bottom on the arm of the lavish settee with the plump, squashy cushions that her parents had bought her as a moving-in present when she took over her warehouse apartment. She lit a cigarette and worried about her friend who seemed as impressionable as ever. 'Have you asked him about this?' she added, blowing smoke rings to calm herself.

There was a pause, then, 'No,' Caitlin said in a small voice. 'Would you bring up the subject of a former wife if you were with a guy who really, really turned you on?'

'Probably,' Saskia returned, adding acerbically, 'Men are rats and I don't suppose Tristan's an exception. I'd want to know his history before cutting to the chase. Don't sell yourself short, girl. Who gave you this idea that you're not amazingly, blazingly gorgeous? How many men have you had over the past few weeks? At least four, isn't it? You must be doing something right.'

'I guess, and I'm so glad you're coming down,' Caitlin said breathily. 'You see something has happened.'

'You're up the duff.'

'No, no . . . though . . . we get on fine, like the same things and all that and . . . he's asked me to get engaged to him.'

Saskia sat there stock-still, doubts and warnings doing double somersaults in her head. Never one to choose her words carefully, she tried to do so now, knowing that if she said the wrong thing it would only make Caitlin even more determined to embark on a course that sounded fraught with danger and difficulties.

'Well, just a cotton-picking minute,' she began, trying to make a joke of it. 'Hold on there. I don't know about an engagement but there's no way you can marry until, I think, seven years after the former partner has been missing, when he/she is presumed dead. Go steady, Caitlin. Tristan needs proof that she really has gone for ever.'

'I know all that.' Caitlin sounded distressed. 'But he says he'll step up the search for her, find her and divorce her for desertion, or reopen the enquiries about her suspected death. There's nothing to stop me accepting his proposal, is there?'

'Well, no, but wait till I get there and we'll talk further. I want to meet this dream-boat of yours, and the other hunks who'll be going begging now you want to plight your troth elsewhere.'

'Please reserve your judgement. He really is a fine person,' Caitlin said, and Saskia promised to keep an open mind.

'Your friend doesn't like me,' Tristan said, after he and Saskia had fenced around each other during dinner.

'She's just overprotective, that's all,' Caitlin answered hurriedly, alarmed by his scowl. She wished she had never asked Saskia to visit and certainly regretted discussing the situation with her.

It was with a certain trepidation that she had arranged for them to dine at High Tides on Friday evening. For one thing, he hadn't been keen, and for another she was all too aware that Raff would be cooking the meal and, though she'd not repeated culinary sex with him, his attitude towards her was a tad impertinent. Yet she was eager to show off her hotel, wanting Tristan and Saskia to be impressed by the way in which it was run, even though it was mostly thanks to Belle.

The manageress had been at table with them for

she was more of a friend than an employee and Caitlin wanted her to meet Saskia and perhaps alter her opinion regarding Tristan. Now, Belle had gone off to the bar with her, and Caitlin was very much afraid that Saskia would be picking her brains with regard to Tristan. She had retreated to her apartment with him and this, too, was a first, as he had never entered, let alone spent a night, in her suite. After evenings out they always ended up at Lyons Court, his lair and bolthole where, presumably, he felt safe.

'She is quick to judge, your friend,' he remarked edgily, prowling the room like a caged tiger, obviously uneasy.

'Not really.' Caitlin rushed to her defence. 'It's just that she worries about me. She's worldly and I'm not.'

'That's why I love you,' he said, and came to rest on the couch, drawing her closer to him and smoothing her hair back from her temples with tender fingertips. 'You're honest and sincere.'

'But not wildly irresistible, like Portia,' she could not help replying.

'Portia was entirely different,' he said, pulling away.

'I know. Robert has told me all about her: what a great hostess she was, how vivacious and charming, and how no one, but *no one*, could ever take her place.'

She recalled how upset she had been when that urbane, perfectly mannered servant had taken her aside during one of her visits, conducted her round and shown her photographs of Portia. He had even unlocked the room that had once been hers, opening wardrobes and drawers and reverently lifting out the exquisite garments she had left behind.

'She had such flair, such beauty and panache,' he had continued, staring at Caitlin with his reptilian eyes. 'Tristan idolised her. He was inconsolable when she disappeared and has never recovered from it, even though there was speculation as to whether he had committed a crime of passion, driven mad by jealousy.'

'Do you think that is true?' she had asked outright, her skin crawling at the way he was speaking to her and his strange, mocking smile.

'That's not for me to say, Miss Colbert,' he had replied and taken her from the room and locked the door. 'But I'll tell you one thing: he'll never be happy with anyone else, nor she with him.'

But now she was here with Tristan, in her own home. She wanted so much that he would share her bed, sleeping with her all night so that she might wake in the morning with him beside her. Whenever she stayed at Lyons Court, she was aware of Robert's presence somewhere in the old house, and was torn between wanting to have breakfast with her lover, and having him drive her back to Queensbury.

As if picking up on her thoughts, Tristan said, 'I'll be leaving soon.'

'Must you go?' She tried not to turn it into a reproach.

'Yes. Besides, you'll want to have a girly gossip with Saskia, no doubt,' he returned.

She wound her arms round his neck and pressed her body against his, kissing the side of his cheek and murmuring, 'We could try out my bed first.'

She knew she was winning when he turned his face towards her and took possession of her mouth, his tongue first running across her lips then, as they parted and softened, entering the warm, wet cavern. Her own tongue met his, caressing and welcoming it. She was certain she had won when she felt the hardening of his cock, and the way in which his hand pushed aside her wrap-over bodice and fastened on her breast. There was no turning back now and, leaving a trail of clothing behind them, they reached the bedroom, still embracing.

They let go of each other long enough to discard the rest of their apparel. Caitlin dropped her panties and lay on the bed, and Tristan hopped on one foot, then the other as he removed his shoes and socks, then peeled down his trousers. Olive-skinned and muscular, she never tired of seeing him naked. As he came to her, his erection swaying slightly, she opened her arms and spread her legs and absorbed him into herself.

He seemed impatient to enter her that night, as if he were re-establishing possession. She arched her back and nudged his hip with her thigh, in an open invitation to explore her, to rub her bud, suck it into his mouth and bring her to roaring orgasm. He ignored her signals, immediately driving his condom-covered organ into her. His entry was forceful, almost painful, though she was wet and slippery. He thrust harder and deeper and she couldn't even get a hand down to her clit to massage it.

She was suddenly reminded of when she had lost her virginity to a selfish young man ignorant of what a woman needed. It was like cold water dousing her sexual fire. Until then, Tristan had always been considerate, bringing her off and then taking his own pleasure. What had happened to change that?

Wildly, she ground her pubis against his cock root, but it missed her clit by a mile. This made her angry and she met his deepening strokes, angling her core this way and that but to no avail. However the friction of his skin and the way his balls banged against the area between her vulva and her anus, gave her a new awareness. Suddenly she wanted to submit to this dominant male, to be a passive thing lying there for him to use.

Fast and furious he plunged in and out of her, not taking his weight on his knees but lying on top of her, braced on straight arms. She knew when he came, felt him pump into the latex that lay between his skin and hers, and then he collapsed, shaking, squashing her into the mattress.

She wondered if he was angry, who he was angry with and whether he might apologise, roll off and lavish care and attention on her clit and give her an orgasm. Instead he got up and started to dress. She propped herself up on one elbow, staring at him, hurt and resentful.

'So that's it, is it?' she said coldly.

'Time for me to go,' he replied, zipping up his trousers.

'What's so urgent?' she asked.

He paused, resting a hand on the brass bed-post, saying, 'You know that I want to marry you?'

'So you've said, but how can you when you aren't yet free of Portia? Saskia asked me what we were going to do about that.'

'I'm sure she did,' he commented sarcastically.

'Portia is the reason why I'm leaving you for a while.'

'You're what?' She rose to her knees on the bed.

'I've had a lead. According to Robert, Portia, or someone very like her, has been seen in London. I'm driving there at the crack of dawn. If I find her, then I'll start divorce proceedings. I'm doing it for us.'

'Is that true? Won't you want her back? You loved her . . . you still love her, don't you?'

He stood rooted to the spot, staring at her with his brows drawn and his eyes as cold as the North Sea. 'Loved her? Yes, I loved her in the beginning, but ended up loathing her.'

With that, he left Caitlin who sank back against the pillows, more confused than ever, her skin prickling, her mind filled with dire presentiments. What had he meant by that last statement? And if he hated Portia so much, was it possible that he had destroyed her? Was his reason for travelling to London simply a red herring?

'You're right. He's gorgeous, but what a dark horse!' Saskia opined when she popped her head round Caitlin's door a while later. 'Belle thinks so, too.'

'You didn't tell her we're engaged?' Caitlin shot up in bed and glared at her.

'You should know me better than that. Would I discuss your personal affairs with her? She's OK, and seems genuinely fond of you, but there are some things that should be kept under wraps.' She flopped down on the quilt, adding, 'And when am I going to meet the rest of your harem? Is Raff in the kitchen right this minute? What's to stop us paying him a visit?'

She was wide awake and randy. Though the journey had been tiring, a nap and a shower before dinner had revitalised her. Sparring with Tristan and getting the low-down from Belle had sharpened her wits. As for Caitlin's property? She glanced round the splendid bedroom; every aspect of the hotel had delighted her, so far.

'Must we?' Caitlin answered, shoulders drooping, part concealed by the floral duvet.

'What's up?' Saskia was at once aware and eager to comfort. 'Where's lover-boy? I thought you'd be bang at it.'

To her dismay, Caitlin started to cry. 'He's gone back to Lyons Court and on to London. He said he'd some new information as to where Portia might be. But supposing he finds her and they make it up? Where would that leave me?'

'Cruising shit creek without a paddle, I guess,' Saskia said, pulling a wad of tissues from the box on the side-table and handing them over. 'Or does it? You might be well shot.'

'He assured me that he loves me and wants us to be free to marry,' Caitlin said. 'That he'll divorce her or, if she doesn't turn up, start fresh enquiries. He loved her once, but ended up hating her.'

'And you believe him?'

'What else can I do? I'm angry, I admit, and fearful of what will happen should they meet.'

Caitlin's woebegone expression moved Saskia deeply. She wanted to hold her and kiss her and comfort her, but was wise enough to recognise this as part genuine concern and part lust. She still fostered the ambition to be Caitlin's first lesbian lover, but now was not the moment.

'I'm sure he'd still dislike her if they met now.

And if not, well, good riddance. Now, cheer up,' she said briskly. 'How about a drink? I see you've had them put a bottle of champagne in my room. Nice touch. Shall I fetch it?'

Caitlin shook her head and dabbed at her eyes. 'Can we catch up in the morning?' she asked. 'I'm shattered. I'll take you to meet the boys then, if it's all right with you.'

'Cool,' Saskia said, shrugging her shoulders and making for the door. As she reached it, she turned to look at Caitlin, 'Listen. If Tristan and you work out, then I'm happy for you. But you're still so young. My advice is to go out and experiment – live a lot more before you settle down.' She smiled. 'Good night, darling. You've a wonderful place here. I envy you.

She walked through the sitting-room and let herself out, deciding to call it a day, retreat to her bedroom down the corridor, then lie in bed, flick on the telly and masturbate to late-night viewing. There might be a soft porn movie on Channel 5, and she never travelled far without her favourite vibrators.

Caitlin took the worn, rough-hewn steps that led to the cove adjacent to High Tides. It was a glorious day with a few puffy white clouds in a picture-postcard sky, the rockbound coast stretching away, throwing out towering projections, with fangs meeting the flowing tide. She watched the dancing wave-crests and listened to the ocean's song, thinking how well Debussy had captured it in his tone poem for orchestra, *La Mer*.

She wasn't the only one enjoying the spectacle. Some of the hotel's guests had already discovered its beauty and settled themselves in sheltered nooks, spreading out towels and opening picnic baskets. A few had braved the elements, dashing into the Atlantic ocean that never warmed, even during a heatwave.

Caitlin continued downwards, then her toes sank in the dry sand and she wandered along the beach, heading in the direction of Tristan's cove, no longer a forbidden paradise. Gulls glided and dived, quarrelsome and noisy, landing on scraps discarded by the holidaymakers lolling on the sand. Caitlin walked on, finally rounding the natural bastion that protected Tristan's domain and ignoring the sign warning that it was out of bounds to unauthorised persons.

Her spirits lifted, although she was missing him dreadfully. True to her word, she had taken Saskia to Banan's studio earlier on, and left her in the company of this artist who was devoted to women, loving their minds as well as their bodies. His portrait of Caitlin had impressed Saskia, and he had asked her if she would let him sketch her. Caitlin and she had shared a conspiratorial smile and he had promised to look after her and deliver her safely to the beach in a while.

'I shall be on Tristan's private one,' she had reminded.

'OK, honey. I'll find you as long as you promise that I'll not be attacked by his bloodhounds.'

'You've been listening to too much gossip,' she had responded tartly.

Now she waded in the shallows, picking her way through bladder wrack, driftwood, crabs and the flotsam and jetsam that gave forth such an aromatic odour. A deep pool glinted at the base of a rocky heap that had fallen from the cliff during some earthquake earlier in the world's history. The water was transparent, sunshine rippling among the small molluscs clinging to the sides and pebbly floor. Leaving shorts, T-shirt and tote bag on a dry boulder, and wearing the three triangles that constituted her bikini, she waded in. The water reached her thighs and it was cold, making her nipples crimp and her pussy ache. She dipped in a hand, seeing how the droplets sparkled on her tanned skin, happy as a child.

Then a shadow passed between her and the sun, and a voice said, 'Good morning, Miss Colbert.'

She spun round, shaded her eyes and stared at the stranger. A serpent had invaded her Eden and she resented him. 'Do I know you?' she demanded bluntly, glad that she hadn't yielded to the impulse to paddle in the pool starkers.

He moved so that the sun no longer threw him into silhouette. He was a lean, good-looking man whose bearing reminded her of Tristan, a mien and way of speaking that was a heritage from public school. He was tall, though not as tall as her lover, and his hair was razor-cut, very stylish, the work carried out in an expensive salon. It was fair, almost white, suggesting long exposure to the bleaching rays of a hot, tropical sun rather than highlights combed through by a coiffeur. He was naked to the waist, his lawn shirt draped over one shoulder, a finger hooked under the collar. And he was coppery brown, with an all-year-round tan that suggested time spent in Florida or Bermuda or the South of France, anywhere frequented by the jet set.

His features had a film-star regularity but it was

144

his eyes that mesmerised her – extraordinarily powerful and persuasive. They were pale blue, with a cold, clear, beautiful glitter that forced her to look at him. Goose-pimples stippled her skin, and her cunt responded to the sexuality of the man. Sakia's advice to experiment more before settling down sprang to mind.

He raised one eyebrow in a sharply quizzical arch. 'We haven't been formally introduced, but I know all about you,' he drawled, and she was tempted to fold an arm across her breasts and cup a hand modestly round the pouch that barely contained her mound. 'You want to know my name? I'm Guy Marlow – Portia's cousin.'

Caitlin stiffened. 'Do you know where she is?'

'No. I haven't been in touch with her since she left here.'

'Oh,' was all she could get out, then waded to where it was easier to leave the pool with a modicum of dignity. He followed her as she reached a boulder, spread out her towel and sat down, letting the hot rays dry her legs and pubic area. Her bikini briefs were soaking, the narrow string gusset cutting between her labial wings.

Guy leaned against another rock, his bare feet crossed at the ankles, the light forming a nimbus round his head, giving him an unearned aura of holiness. Caitlin was sure he was a far cry from sainthood.

'Robert was right,' he said suddenly, slanting her a glance. 'He told me that you were pretty.'

This jolted her into immediate suspicion. 'Robert Vintner? Tristan's manservant?'

'That's right.'

'You know him? Keep in touch with him?

Tristan has never mentioned you. How come?'

Guy's smile did not reach his eyes. 'Tristan doesn't like me.'

'Why not?'

'Ah, dear child, that's a long story and I want to talk about pleasanter things ... you, for starters. Tell me all about yourself.'

'There's not much to tell. I've led a quiet, boring existence until just lately,' she replied, but in spite of her resolution to keep him in ignorance, he had the power to draw her out and was soon in possession of her early life and most recent experiences. She had the presence of mind not to mention her amatory adventures, but had the feeling that he knew anyway. As she spoke she was aware that his presence aroused her, and she was sure her tiny bikini did little to hide this.

Suddenly he moved closer, stood behind her and slipped a hand over her shoulder, dipping down to cradle her right breast under its flimsy covering. Sensation darted through her as he rolled his thumb over her nipple. It was so acute that she gasped aloud. She could feel him laughing, his warm bare chest pressed against her naked skin.

'I think you've been a naughty girl,' he purred in her ear, sending chills down her spine. 'Not exactly telling me the truth. I know different, you see. I've heard that you've been bonking like an alley cat, starting with Banan, then having a poke with Jon, and playing at chef with Raff ... to say nothing of Tristan.'

'What do you mean?' She found it hard to talk, flooded with guilt as if caught out by a stern headmaster. And her nipple burned at his skilled touch

146

and the gusset of her tanga was wet with more than just seawater.

'Rather you should ask, how do I know? Everything that happens in and around Lyons Court is reported back to me,' he said, and his tender caress turned to a pinch. She yelped, yet wanted more. He released her abruptly, adding, 'I think we'll pay a visit to the old place, don't you?'

'But Tristan's not there. He said I could use it and the cove, but not you.'

'No problem. Come with me. Never mind about putting on your shorts and top. Put them in your bag.'

It wasn't exactly fear she was experiencing, more curiosity about this intriguing man. He had alerted her body to a need for new sensations. She responded to the way he spoke, that commanding manner, and to this was added an imp of perversity all her own. She was angry because Tristan had gone away, no matter how reasonable his excuse. And, as she walked up the winding, tree-shaded path that led to his home, she was very aware that it wasn't his fingers linked with hers, or his hand skimming lightly over her bare shoulders and, serve him right, she thought childishly. I'm consorting with his enemy.

This rebellious feeling continued when they entered the Great Hall to be greeted by Robert who was falling all over himself to please Guy. This is the one, she thought, the spy in the camp, the maggot in the apple. Tristan had said he had been part of Portia's entourage and must have kept in touch with her cousin. He was behaving most oddly, obsequious one moment and bold the next, almost flirting with him.

'So you found her,' he said, with an arch smile.

'Oh, yes, and now I think it's time to give her an insight into how things were during the time Portia lived here with Tristan. Is there anyone else in the house?'

'No, sir. The daily cleaners have left, and we don't employ indoor staff when Mr Trevellyan is away.'

'Good. I want to open our guest to pleasures she hasn't yet tasted. To me she's still a virgin in certain respects.'

Feeling out of place and very exposed in her bikini and leaving sandy footprints on the oak flooring, Caitlin permitted herself to be led to that part of the house once occupied by Portia. In a way, she was thankful that Robert had already acquainted her with the apartment. He unlocked the cedarwood door and stood back so that she and Guy might enter. As before, the rooms had an unused smell, though someone, and she presumed it to be Robert, had opened the diamond-paned windows. Flowers stood in magnificent vases, Star-Gazer lilies that breathed out a strong perfume, ferns and waxy, heavily scented stephanotis.

'I like to keep it just as it was when she was here,' Robert said raptly, and Caitlin realised the depths of his obsession with Portia.

'I'm sure she would appreciate your concern, but now there's a new woman, one that I intend to initiate,' Guy answered, and threw his shirt over the back of a delicate gilded Louis-Quatorze chair.

Robert seemed not to have heard him, disappearing into a closet near the en suite bathroom. Caitlin went to the window, looking down over gardens that the outdoor staff kept to perfection. It was weird to imagine Portia standing there, day after day, mistress of all she surveyed.

'Glorious, isn't it?' said Guy from behind her and his hands cupped her buttocks, one finger pushing aside her G-string and delving into her crack. She closed her eyes, shivering.

He lifted her hair and nuzzled the nape of her neck. She could feel his erection surging behind his trousers and could not resist arching her bottom against it. She knew she shouldn't be enjoying it, but that made her want it more. Guy was a challenge, awakening her to dark desires she hadn't even known she possessed.

She loved Tristan, but had to agree when Guy murmured silkily, 'He's quite conventional in his lovemaking, isn't he? That's what Portia always said. A bit of a dry old stick ... didn't like to experiment. Have you found this to be so?'

'Not at all,' she lied loyally.

'Now, now ... you can tell me ...' and he twirled her round to face him, making her even more aware of his cock that swelled almost to his waistband. His flaxen chest hair tickled her breasts, and that of his armpits was redolent of arousing male body odour masked by costly anti-perspirants.

She stared into his unfathomable eyes and said, 'I don't have to. You have no business being here.'

'Doesn't that make it all the more thrilling?' And, as he spoke, his agile fingers slipped the knots each side of her tanga and it fell away, exposing her mound to his gaze.

He stared down at her flat, tanned belly and part-shaven pubis. She started back, but wanted him to go further. She knew she should retrieve her bikini, gather up her belongings and leave, but she was no more capable of doing this than she was of stopping breathing.

Instead, she lifted her chin defiantly and said, 'You may as well see the rest,' then yanked off her top.

To her amazement, fury crossed his face and he gripped her wrists cruelly. 'You shouldn't have done that,' he snarled. 'You must wait till I command you. That way you'll learn to be my submissive and I shall be your master.'

'Are you crazy?'

'I see through you, Caitlin, and beneath that prissy exterior there's a slut-slave longing to get out. I intend to use her, abuse her and bring her to ecstasy.'

This nightmarish scenario intensified when a figure stepped out of the dressing room. Just for a blood-chilling second, Caitlin thought it was Portia, or her ghost, wearing a black chiffon evening gown, very tight and slinky, with a feather boa draped round the shoulders and tangling with the back-brushed russet curls. Splits in the skirt displayed black-stockinged legs as the apparition glided along. The face was heavily made up, a parody of the woman in the portrait.

Guy gave a bellow of laughter, exclaiming, 'Jesus God! You don't look much like Portia.'

Robert did a twirl in front of the pier-glass, tossing back his ringlets coquettishly and staring at Guy under lowered, jade-green lids. 'I think I do,' he announced, fingering his false breasts through the silk bodice. 'It used to amuse her to have me try on her clothes. She taught me a lot about cosmetics and wigs and how to create an illusion.'

'So you still come up here sometimes and get off on wearing her things. Does it turn you on, Robert? Do you wank while you're admiring yourself?'

'Yes, I do. There's nothing so exciting. I've always worn women's clothes, ever since I first discovered my dick. I wanted to be a drag queen. I've even done a few gigs in the gay clubs.'

Guy was watching him with an alert expression, the bulge in his pants even more prominent. 'Jerk off, Robert,' he commanded.

'Yes, master,' Robert lisped, and rubbed the front of his dress where his phallus made a substantial bump.

'Not yet,' Guy shouted, and swept Caitlin up in his arms and deposited her on the ostentatious bed that was draped and lavishly decorated like an eighteenth-century courtesan's.

She was aware of several things at once: the realisation that her nakedness left Robert cold, a sudden flood of apprehension, and the conviction that something amazing was about to happen. Then, with a flick of the wrist, Guy released a mechanism concealed near the top of the bed and chains slithered lose. Guy rolled her over on to her stomach and fastened fur-lined cuffs round her wrists, then clipped them to rings attached to the chains.

He repeated the procedure, shackling her ankles. Her legs were spread wide, a cold draft playing round her slit. There was no way she could shield or protect herself. She cursed her foolhardiness that had landed her in this situation. It was far worse than when Raff had used her as a dinner plate. Guy was as yet an unknown quantity. He could really hurt her, if he had a mind to. There would be nothing she could do to stop him, and she had a shrewd idea that Robert wouldn't come to her aid.

Guy ran his hands all the way down her spine, then wetted a finger in her vulva. She was shocked into yelping when she felt him inserting it into the tiny eyelet of her back passage. Why did some men lust to explore this forbidden region? Raff had wanted to try it, too. What would it feel like, she wondered, to have this very private place invaded?

He did not withdraw his finger, but wriggled it in further while she tried to cringe away, prevented by her bonds. She whimpered.

'You're very tight,' he said thoughtfully. 'You've never been buggered, have you?'

'No,' she gasped.

'Not Tristan's thing at all, is it? Well, slave, you'll learn to take it from me. I'll demonstrate the art, and soon have you fitted with butt-plugs to stretch you so that you can accommodate either the male member, or dildos.'

'I won't. You can't make me,' she cried indignantly.

'You must learn to obey me.' He sighed, more in sorrow than anger and, simultaneously, she heard the snap of palm on flesh and felt searing heat shoot through her buttocks.

A thread of salty tears ran down her cheek and

wet the pillow. 'You're cruel,' she said. 'No one has ever slapped me before.'

'There's a first time for everything,' he countered coolly, and hit her again. He stood back, admiring the pink blotches forming on her skin. 'That looks very sweet. I've been careful not to mark you, because you won't be wearing much during this hot spell.'

'I shall tell Saskia about you,' Caitlin threatened, though as the sting of his blows dulled into a sullen fire, she felt the heat communicating with her nipples and clit and wanted him to rub her labial groove and satisfy the climax that was waiting in the wings.

'Ah, so that's her name, your beautiful friend who has come to stay. I saw her today from a distance, and she struck me as the kind of woman who would be up for this . . . spankings, floggings and arse fucking. You will introduce us.'

A vivid picture of Saskia leapt into her mind, strung out as she now was, helpless in the master's hands. This was so arousing that she ground her pubis into the mattress, trying to bring pressure to bear on her clit. She heard Guy move and braced herself instinctively, afraid of him and what he might do. There was a swish and the impact of a flexible object against the backs of her thighs. She jerked, tugging at her restricted wrists and ankles. In the next moment Guy appeared within her sight, holding out a small paddle covered in white leather. He laid it swiftly against his palm where it twanged then sprang back.

'This is a tool for novices, like yourself,' he explained. 'I have many more delightful toys that you will become acquainted with all in good time.'

To her relief he freed her limbs and had her lie on her back, running his hands over every inch of her and lingering between her labia, teasing and tormenting her engorged bud. He bent and closed his mouth on one nipple, sucking until it was almost twice its size. Then he transferred this attention to the other, while Caitlin used her fingers on the wet teat he had just abandoned.

'You want to be satisfied?' he murmured.

'Yes, I do. You know I do,' she sobbed, forgetting shame in the urgency of her body's demands.

Grasping her firmly by the hips, he tongued her clitoris. She dug her nails in his white-blond hair and pulled him closer to her crotch. She felt the pleasure waves gathering in her groin and gave a hoarse cry. He tore himself free of her and stood up. Shocked and disappointed, on the very brink of coming, she jabbed a hand down to her slippery wet organ that was pulsating and throbbing.

He grabbed her hand away, shouting, 'No! You don't do that till I give my permission. Lie there and watch and learn.'

She had wanted to see his penis, but he had remained half dressed, till now. With a lithe movement, he turned from her, unzipped, and released his large, fair-skinned tool. The light danced off the ring that pierced it. She gazed at it for a moment, then he kicked off his trousers and beckoned to Robert. The manservant sank to his knees in front of him and reverently covered that stiff piece of equipment and its gilded jewellery with a flesh-coloured condom.

'That was well done, slave,' Guy growled, his cock so hard and huge that it reached his navel. 'Bend over.'

Robert obeyed, turning his back to Guy and going down from the waist after hitching his skirt high over his skinny rump. He wore scarlet silk knickers and a garter belt with suspenders clipped to his stocking tops. His legs were long and shapely, the muscles accentuated by his stiletto heels. Guy peeled down the panties, then leaned across and dipped his fingers in a jar of Vaseline on the bedside table and applied it to the silvery-pink latex that protected his cock. Another scoop was pushed up and lost in the dark rosette of Robert's anus.

Caitlin guessed what he was going to do next and would have averted her eyes if she could, but found the prospect of watching them disturbing yet fascinating. She had sometimes wondered how men did it with one another. She was about to find out.

Robert's hindquarters intrigued her. He had become androgynous, a creature part female, part male, in black chiffon and feathers, silk underwear with weighty masculine balls dangling between his legs, a cock jutting out front and a lubricated arse hole.

And the naked Guy pleased her eyes and senses, so well built, golden fair, and with a body like a Greek god's. He smiled grimly, picked up a deerskin flogger and brought it down across Robert's right buttock. Robert jerked and groaned but remained bent over, his hands clasped round his ankles. Guy lashed his other bum cheek, a lattice of red strips marking the white skin. Robert sighed and moaned. Guy hit him again.

'No more, master, I beg you,' Robert pleaded, but without conviction.

Guy gave him another half a dozen lashes, by which time Robert was holding his erection and rubbing it vigorously. Guy reached round and handled his slave's balls, then fingered the cock, brushing Robert's hand aside. Robert lurched, cried out and came, his spunk spattering the carpet at his feet.

'You've enjoyed your whipping far too much,' Guy snapped, and pushed forward between Robert's legs, then thrust his tool all the way into the prepared orifice.

'Oh,' Robert sighed. 'Oh, yes, master ... fuck me, fuck me.'

Guy braced his knees to give him greater purchase and moved faster and faster, his cock sliding in and out of Robert's well-used passage, appearing and disappearing, his balls slapping against Robert's own. His eyes cut to Caitlin.

'Do it now,' he commanded. 'Bring yourself off.'

She needed no second bidding, spreading her legs open and fingering her wet cleft, then, while watching the two men humping, rubbing her clit forcefully. The feeling that had hovered on the periphery since Guy had sucked and aroused her, now started to build steadily. It was rising, mounting, just as Guy's ejaculation was gathering in his balls, ready to explode. With each powerful thrust, Robert moved a little way forward, still leaning over, still gripping his ankles.

Seeing these two at it, feverish with excitement, made Caitlin incredibly horny. They were both panting as if they were running a marathon, then Guy gave a final, savage thrust and stopped, and she knew he had reached his zenith. Her knees went weak, her clit spasmed and she screamed as her climax overcame her.

CHAPTER

8

'I couldn't get through to you today,' Tristan said down the phone, and the reproach in his voice made Caitlin squirm. If he knew what she had been doing!

'I was on the beach and had my mobile switched off,' she replied, thinking, that's half the story anyway. 'I'm in charge of the hotel tonight. Belle's gone out. It's getting easier for me to keep everything together. Mr Ramsey is a treasure and Saskia is staying, so she'll help. How are things going up there? Any sign of Portia?'

'No,' he answered gloomily. 'The private eye I hired is worse than useless. Costs me a bomb and doesn't come up with anything. I'm replacing him with someone else. He reckoned she'd been seen in Harrod's, and he'd heard that she was living somewhere on the outskirts of London, but nothing concrete. I'm staying in the Chelsea flat. It's so hot and oppressive in town and I miss Cornwall. I want to come home and long to see you, darling, but I'll give it a couple more days.'

How was it that the pain gnawing inside her because they were separated seemed to have lessened? Could she be so fickle that the appearance of a new, fascinating man had totally thrown her? She fingered the bruises on her thighs; they weren't dark, just a bit pinker than the surrounding skin, and as she did so, her wayward clit remembered and throbbed and her nipples puckered, tender against her lacy brassière.

'I'm missing you,' she whispered, and she was – in a way.

'Me too, but if it means I can put the past well and truly behind me, then it will have been worth it.' He was so matter-of-fact, and Caitlin couldn't help recalling the things Guy had said about him, cruel, dismissive things, like that he was boring, staid and unwilling to explore the dark byways of passion.

'Do you miss me in bed?' she asked, dropping her voice to a huskier level. 'I think about you at night and play with myself under the duvet.' She was surprised by her boldness, knowing she had Guy to thank for it.

'Is that so?' Tristan sounded intrigued.

'Oh, yes. I'm sitting in my room now, with my hand in my panties. It's so warm and wet there and I wish it was your finger parting my cleft and rubbing my little button, just like I'm doing at this moment.' This was no fairytale; even as she spoke, she was carrying out the actions.

There was silence down the other end of the phone, then he said, 'Are you really doing that?'

'Yes,' she said unsteadily. 'One hand is between my legs, then I dart up and fondle my tits, backwards and forwards. I smell so fruity.'

'You're really masturbating?' His voice went lower. She wondered if he was stroking his cock. Even in their most intimate moments, she had been too shy to inquire if he jacked off.

'Yes, and it's oh-so sweet.'

'What are you thinking about?' His voice was deeper still.

'You, and how I'd like to perform for you . . . like a pole dancer. I'd rouge my nipples and ride a huge dildo. You could watch it slipping in and out of me. I want to flaunt my tits in your face and have you reach out to kiss them.'

'Caitlin! That isn't like you!' There was astonishment in his voice, but he was breathing harder.

'We haven't been together long, Tristan. How well do you know me? Listen to my fingers slurping in and out of my snatch,' and she held the phone to her crotch. 'Can you hear it, all juicy for me?' He was beginning to gasp and she added, 'Have you got your prick out? Are you rubbing it, up and down the stem, then squeezing the tip and lubricating it from the eye?' He didn't answer and she went on, triumphantly, 'You are, aren't you? Oh, how I wish I was there. I'd suck it and milk you dry.'

The pictures conjured by her words made the hot blood surge through her, and her swollen clit poised on the edge of repletion. A few more strokes and she would be there, but she wanted to do it with him, imagining him in an apartment she had never seen, slumped in a leather chair, his long legs spread, his jeans unbuttoned and his shapely cock jerking between his furiously working fingers.

'Are you coming? Is it getting too much for you?' she whispered. 'Tell me how hard you are. Think of me with my knickers down, and my pussy all ready for you.'

'God!' he gasped. 'All right. Yes, I'm rubbing myself.'

He sounded so hot. Caitlin could almost see his phallus throbbing in front of her, smell it and taste the strong, salty flavour of his jism. 'Good. Describe what you're feeling,' she demanded, in command now, not touching her clit, letting her finger rest just above it.

'Oh, it's great . . . I can almost feel your touch on it, Caitlin. And see your lovely hole and feel it closing round me like a velvet glove. Ahhh . . . ahhh . . . I can't hold back,' and he gave a harsh cry, and she visualised a fountain of semen spraying his thighs and belly and trousers.

She came, panting as hard as he was, then muttering, 'Oh, Tristan, I wish I was there to lick you clean.'

'I'll be with you soon,' he gasped, then his voice steadied as the spasms subsided. 'I'll ring you tomorrow, darling.'

'Well, here's a turn-up for the books,' Saskia remarked when, over dinner, Caitlin told her about her encounter with Guy and subsequent events. 'I want to meet him.'

'That can be arranged, but we'll have to do it before Tristan comes back. Guy will be gone by then.'

'How about tonight, when you've shut up shop?' Saskia suggested.

'OK. I'll ring him and we can drive over, but it won't be till around midnight.'

'Mr Ramsey will hold the fort, won't he?'

'Yes, and Belle is expected back by then.'

Saskia was queening it in the dining area and foyer. The guests seemed to like her, even though, unlike Caitlin, who wore a plain and simple dress, she had opted for the eccentric and fashionable 'distressed' look. One lace-edged sleeve of her pink tulle bodice was ripped down over her shoulder, and the rosette that decorated it hung by a couple of threads. Her breasts were made more prominent by a strapless boob tube worn beneath, and her broderie anglaise skirt was full, like a Victorian petticoat, pink to match the top, and equally tattered. There were three hundred pounds' worth of strappy sandals on her feet, and the rest of her gear had set Daddy back a further four hundred.

The clients found her engaging in the same way that they were titillated by Banan's Bohemian lifestyle and appearance. Something they might have liked to have done, yet were too hide-bound to ever attempt. She played to the gallery, vivacious and alluring, making the women envious and the men struggle to control their erections.

'And how is Banan?' Caitlin asked when, clientele settled in restaurant or guestrooms, they took a coffee break.

A warm, lubricious sensation bathed Saskia's plushy depths at the mention of his name. She had never imagined for one moment that she would find such a lover buried in the countryside. 'Banan is stupendous,' she answered, lighting up a cigarette; they were sitting on the terrace, well away from the other diners. 'He can stay in my flat when he comes to London for art exhibitions. I expect I can put business his way. Are you sure you don't mind us screwing?'

'Not at all,' Caitlin answered with a smile. 'I realised that it was never going to be an on-going thing with us. Great fun while it lasted, and I'm not saying we shan't do it again in the future, but just for now ... I've enough on my plate with Tristan and Guy.'

'I'm intrigued to try out Raff and Jon,' Saskia confessed, never satisfied with one lover, or maybe afraid to get too involved, too fond and too vulnerable. She had sworn that love wasn't for her – not yet – not for ages – maybe never. She had witnessed the havoc it had wreaked amongst her friends.

She had seen Raff in the kitchens, sized up his equipment (and this wasn't his knives and skillets), and peeked at Jon through his shop door. Beards turned her on, and he gave the impression of being a Viking warrior. She had time enough and to spare during which to test out these two splendid men. She had finished one assignment for her interior designer boss, and there was a lull until they started the next commission. And now there was another challenge in the form of the devilish and intriguing Guy.

'Did you ring him, Caitlin?' she asked, her cigarette tip glowing in the dark blue dimity of the garden. The sky was streaked with orange on the horizon where the sun had dipped out of sight.

'I did and he has ordered me to bring you to him.'

'Ordered, eh? Very much the dominating master. I've met his kind before. Don't be intimidated. Use him for your pleasure, enjoy everything

162

he does, pain and all. In that way the roles will be confused. Who is master and who submissive?'

'You've taken part in this?'

'I've been associated with the scene. Leather and PVC, bondage straps and whips,' and as she talked of it and remembered, Saskia could feel her cunt getting moist and that familiar heaviness gathering in her groin. 'What are we waiting for? Let's go,' and she ground her stub out under her heel.

Caitlin hesitated, seemed reluctant to speak, then blurted out, 'He wants to take me up the back passage. He talks about using butt-plugs, and inserting dildos in my bottom. Does it hurt? Have you had it done to you?'

Saskia wanted to giggle at her alarmed expression. She looked as if she was clenching her buttocks at the very thought of penetration. The soft light of the overhead lanterns bathed her and, despite her black dress and hair screwed into a bun, she still looked like a girl playing at dressing-up, borrowing her mother's clothes. Banan had remarked on her pretty face and naïve mannerisms.

Saskia slipped a hand under Caitlin's arm and paced with her into reception. 'There isn't much I haven't tried in the sex Olympics,' she said, reassuringly. 'And being buggered is certainly one of them.'

Caitlin shuddered and said in a hushed voice, 'But it sounds so dirty. I don't see that I'd ever enjoy it.'

'Don't knock it until you've tried,' Saskia advised, tingling at the notion that she might soon witness Guy pushing his tool into Caitlin's deepest, darkest and most private orifice. 'Think about it.'

'I have and I don't like the idea. Raff was interested and Guy certainly is. I'm sure he'll want to do it to me soon. I'm afraid it will hurt.'

'It may, at first, but you'd be surprised at the thrill it can give. A big cock shoved right up your jacksy.'

Caitlin stopped in the middle of the tiled floor. 'I've changed my mind,' she declared. 'I don't want to go to Lyons Court.'

'Don't be a chicken,' Saskia said, unwilling to have her turn stubborn, change her mind and refuse to take her. Guy sounded the most tremendous fun – rogue, cad and con man though he might very well be. The bad boys were always the most exciting.

'I'm not,' Caitlin said mulishly. 'It's just that this seems so unnatural . . . rude and disgusting.'

'Look at it another way,' Saskia said softly, steering her through the glass panelled lobby door, and towards a car to bear them to their destination. 'As primitive man evolved, so did happy sensations that occurred in the brain whenever a life sustaining body function was performed. So, everyone was encouraged to eat to the full, sleep, pee, shit and so forth.'

'I still don't get it.

'You're all right with kissing, aren't you? Well, the mouth's a good example. Kissing produces an euphoric chemical reaction because our bodies think we're eating. The nipples are the same, and the anus when used for sex. Clinically, there's no difference between stimulation of the mouth, ears, tits and arsehole in the production of those pleasurable feelings in the cortex.'

'I thought it was illegal,' Caitlin persisted.

'Arse fucking is accepted in some places, but not in others. A number of American states are twitchy about it and people have been imprisoned, even if they were doing it within marriage.'

'I'm still not convinced,' Caitlin said, shaking her head as they got into the Mercedes and she pressed the ignition button.

Lyons Court was well lit, with security lights on everywhere, and Caitlin steered the car round to the back where Guy had told her that Robert would be waiting to let them in. Saskia immediately summed him up as a slimy toad, very much out for his own gain, but was prepared to go along with his exaggerated air of friendliness for the time being.

'I expect you'd like to go through the Great Hall and show it to Miss Higgins,' he said to Caitlin, leading the way. 'It really is a unique house.'

'Stunning,' Saskia conceded, and she meant it. She had visited some fine old stately homes in her time, but this Cornish manor surpassed them. She could see why Caitlin might fancy herself as its mistress; indeed she would probably have thought twice about it, had its owner offered. But it was really too remote for her, as was the whole of the peninsula; fine for a holiday, but she needed the roar and bustle of the city.

But she forgot this when a door opened at the end of a passage upstairs and she went into the softly lit splendour of an exquisitely furnished suite.

'This was Portia's apartment,' Caitlin whispered.

Saskia saw the blond man standing in the centre of the lavishly splendid room. He wore a long purple velvet robe that added to his considerable height. His cold eyes met hers, and she steeled herself to return his penetrating gaze. She'd met his type before and was not intimidated, only aroused.

'Caitlin,' he said in cultured accents that Saskia recognised. Most of her life had been spent among people who spoke like that.

'Master,' Caitlin whispered, head down, eyes on the floor, her hands locked behind her. 'This is Saskia.'

He snapped his fingers at Robert who filled three crystal flutes with champagne and handed them round. 'Here's to a productive meeting,' Guy said, toasting Caitlin and Saskia over the rim. 'And to a closer association in the future.'

He had a powerful body and the mind of a control freak, and Saskia tingled in anticipation of an interesting evening. He put down his glass and said, 'Strip.'

Caitlin tried to hide behind Saskia while she, holding his stare and thrusting out her breasts, replied tauntingly, 'I only do it to music.'

His smile became taut, his eyes excited. He jerked a thumb towards the hi-fi and Robert flipped through the discs, finding a suitable one. The music started – a throbbing, bump and grind beat – and Saskia went through her routine, one that she had perfected when performing at wild parties. She knew just how to give a tantalising glimpse of bare flesh, slipping her pink tulle bodice off one shoulder and pulling down the boob tube, revealing a nipple. Eyeing Guy brazenly, she scrutinised his erection, which was so hard and stiff that it poked through the front fastening of his purple robe. The cock ring glittered, the black beads were smeared with pre-come. She imagined the metal rubbing

166

against the lining of her vagina. She removed her bodice and wrinkled the boob tube down to her supple waist, then lifted one leg and placed her stilt-heeled sandalled foot on a chair, her full skirt falling back to display her bare pussy.

'More,' Guy ordered.

Saskia wanted to retort, 'Stuff you!' but carried on playing the game, remembering the rules.

She tossed back her hair with showgirl insolence, and whipped off her pink tube. Her breasts sprang free, full and firm, with darkly pointed nipples that were extra stiff through arousal.

She heard Guy's swift intake of breath and she lowered her leg and let loose the waistband of her skirt. It slithered to the floor and she stood there in her high heels, ribs lifted, arms akimbo, the epitome of the mocking, contemptuous tart. She didn't move as he fingered her, familiarising himself with her breasts, cunt and backside, saying, 'Here's an arse that likes to be abused. You should instruct your friend.'

'We talked of it,' Saskia answered, her flesh burning under his caresses, her hand polishing his superb prick. 'Damn you,' she hissed, and was caught in the down-draught of Caitlin's shock at daring to speak to him so defiantly.

So far, Caitlin had been called upon to do nothing but watch. Now it was her turn.

Guy left Saskia, her hands tethered to the bed-post, with Robert, who was grinning and standing guard over her. Caitlin was still wearing her simple black dress, the one which she thought made her look sophisticated. She had to admit that she no longer felt businesslike and worldly – just scared and excited. She felt Guy behind her and heard the dress's back zip running down. Next moment, it was off, leaving her in bra and panties.

She had seen the way he had played with Saskia and remembered how he had screwed Robert after punishing her. Would she be the recipient of his lust tonight? Without waiting to be told, Robert walked across to one of the mirrors and pressed the edge. At once it sprang open, revealing a cupboard filled with equipment. He reached in and took down a length of heavy chain.

He gave it to Guy who walked across to a small stepladder and fastened one portion of the chain to a hook screwed high in the ceiling. Robert propelled Caitlin towards the chain that now hung vertically, almost reaching the carpet. She was unaccustomed to stack heels and tottered a little, the cool air stippling her skin, and making her nipples crimp under the bra cups. She felt dampness smearing the gusset of her knickers as she moved closer to Guy.

His face was expressionless, but his robe was open wide, displaying his massive cock, ornamented and shining with gold and jism. She stopped in front of him, and he said, 'Lift your hands above your head.'

She obeyed and he snapped a pair of cuffs round her wrists. These were linked together and, when her arms were fully strained upwards, he fastened the heavier chain to them. She swung there, with her toes scraping the floor. He slid his hands under her bra straps and forced the wired baskets below her breasts, which were standing out like two cherry-encrusted globes. Then he bent and kissed them, rolling his tongue round each. Caitlin gasped and strained towards that burning touch, but he withdrew his mouth and pinched them hard. His penis pressed against her belly and he rubbed himself up and down her, leaving a trail of juice. Then his hand was between her legs, ripping off her panties and leaving her pussy bare.

She bit her lip, trying to stay silent and hide her frantic need for him to take her. Guy smiled, undeceived. 'Don't deny it. You're wet. I can feel it. My fingers are slippery with it. Look, and taste,' and he held his hand to her lips and nose. She inhaled the seashore odour of her own essence.

'Now,' he said, and lowered her arms, unhooking them but keeping her wrists bound together. He knelt down and wound the chain round her feet. She could not move her legs.

The feeling was terrifying yet sexy. He reached round and thrust his hand between her tightly closed thighs and she moaned as he spread her lips open and delved into her juices, but didn't apply it to her tormented clit. Then he pushed the small of her back, making her bend over. Next he walked round in front of her and rubbed his cock thoughtfully. The gold shone, the onyx flashed and his helm was fiery red. She thirsted to take it into her mouth. He let her, holding her head steady while he introduced his tip between her lips. It tasted salty, and the skin felt so silky against her tongue.

Caitlin was uncomfortable, yet this was of no consequence compared to the excitement building in her depths. He withdrew, his cock dripping with his emission and her saliva. She felt him move behind her and heard him say, 'You want me, don't you? Your wetness tells me that you can't wait to have me take you, and I'm going to, but not where you expect.'

He paused, waiting for her reaction. 'Oh, no. Not *that*,' she cried and struggled against her bonds to no avail.

'Indeed – *that!*' he echoed, and began to insert a finger into her anus.

'Ow!' she shouted, but he persisted, adding another finger, then smearing her juice around her crack, between her lips and along her rectal aperture.

Before she knew it, his fingers were replaced by something larger, harder, and more brutally insistent. Caitlin moaned, unsure whether she was experiencing intense pain or ravishing pleasure. His prick was rubber-covered, but slippery as silk, and, ignoring her protests, he eased it in, further and further, till she felt herself expanding to take him. It was unlike any other penetration she had ever known and she felt as if she were being stuffed as he slid in deeper and deeper, her rectum throbbing, burning and affording her a strange, forbidden sensation.

'Oh God!' she gasped, every instinct urging her to repel this brutal invader. Then suddenly he achieved his goal, his cock buried to the hilt, his wiry fair bush chafing her bottom.

'Saskia,' he commanded, and Robert released her hands. She came across, and Guy continued, 'Massage her clit. I want to feel her come.'

Caitlin knew that Saskia was on her knees in front of her, and felt her softly parting her swollen lips and caressing her clit. This broke down the final barrier. Waves of desire racked Caitlin so that she was no longer aware of her extended rectum, only of the pleasure Saskia was providing and that odd, compelling rhythm as Guy's hips hollowed and thrust and his cock slid out almost to the glans, then plunged back right up her, filling her to the brim.

She hadn't realised how wonderful a woman's touch on her nubbin could be and lifted her pelvis as far as she could, seeking more contact. Saskia rubbed her gently, and, as Guy plunged and bucked, seeking his fulfilment, so Caitlin reached the mightiest orgasm of her life, yelling as she climaxed. He came, too, in several quick jerks, then pulled away from her and her arse contracted as if wanting to hold on to him, yet glad to see him go.

Saskia was in a ferment of arousal. She had licked Caitlin, tasted her sweet, aromatic juices after watching her milking Guy, her cheeks drawn in by the strength of her sucking. He had endured it, stroking her hair, tickling her clit, but never shedding a single drop of semen. Saskia had been disappointed, wanting to see him fountain his ecstasy between Caitlin's lips, his hips jerking convulsively. This thought had made her grind her thighs together in a vain effort to bring pressure to bear on her bud.

Then he had started arse-fucking Caitlin and ordered Saskia to make her climax for him.

Now, bonds freed, she lay on the bed with Caitlin, caressing her soothingly, and hoping that she would reciprocate and make love to her, inexperienced in lesbianism though she was. She was anticipating the moment when Guy would want to chastise them, certain it would happen. Caitlin had told her that he had spanked her and used a paddle. Saskia guessed that he wanted to progress further but conscious that any marks he left would be visible through their summer clothing, or when they swam or sunbathed, he had to restrain himself.

Robert hung around in the background. He had changed into a frock and an auburn wig, and was pulling up his skirt and fingering himself. Saskia was unfazed; some of her best friends were transvestites, and if he got his kicks watching Guy fucking females, well, so be it. She was sure that Guy would have plenty left over for him: a length of cock, a cane and ten of the best. Whatever floated his boat.

Guy refilled his glass, ice cool once more. Saskia lounged against the pillows and openly admired him and his phallus. Her knowledge of the male appendage was legion. Caitlin cuddled closer to her, and Saskia did what she had hungered to do for months; she placed her hand on Caitlin's mound, hearing her startled gasp and feeling her struggling with her conscience before she gave in to her caress. Then, tentatively at first, her hand touched Saskia's nipples.

'Ah, yes,' Saskia murmured. 'That's right. Do it some more, then rub my clit.'

Caitlin became bolder, her fingers sliding down past Saskia's navel and finding the deep groove that parted her sex. Saskia had no need to guide her. Caitlin was taking to it like a duck to water. Locked mouth to cunt, she brought Saskia off with her lips and tongue. Caitlin had shrugged off her inhibitions, transformed into a thing avid for pleasure, showing no hesitation in going down on Saskia, then bringing her to climax again with her hand. Guy stood over them, his recharged erection bobbing as he ordered them put their slits together, then licked the length of the two. They lay on top of one another as if they were man and woman, and he mouthed all their orifices before putting his latex-protected cock into one pouting cunt, then the other, moving with such speed that his fierce orgasm soon shook them both.

Then he sat on the bed and reached for the pleasure-drugged Caitlin, and she lay across his lap like an obedient slave. Her hair hung down on one side, her breasts were pressed into his naked thigh, and his cock nudged her waist, leaving a silvery trail. Saskia knew he wanted to do more than just spank them, but he restricted himself to putting them over his knee, one after another, and administering brisk blows with his open palm. These stung, but were nothing to Saskia who enjoyed harsher treatment.

Robert brought in more wine and canapés, and Guy lolled on the bed like an emperor surrounded by his concubines. He was replete for the time being, and Saskia took the opportunity of finding out more about him and his intentions regarding Caitlin.

'You only come here when Tristan is away?' she began, caressing the fair fuzz on his chest and running her nails over his hard nipples. 'Did you call in much when Portia was around?'

'Of course, as one does when one has a close cousin. We were inseparable until she met him.'

'You were jealous?'

'Not of their relationship. No one was as close to her as me. Envious of his wealth and this place, perhaps,' and his expansive gesture encompassed the whole house. 'Portia and I had always lived on our wits. Done very well by it, too. Ran through any money we inherited from our parents, and we both think work is beneath us. Why should two such shimmering, godlike beings soil their hands or cudgel their brains simply to feed themselves and keep a roof over their heads?'

'You're a conceited bastard, aren't you?' Saskia said levelly, circling his navel and hairy lower belly, then teasing his semi-flaccid dick. 'And where does Robert slot into the equation?'

'He's besotted with me, aren't you, bitch?' Guy demanded, slapping Robert's buttocks.

'I'm devoted to both of you, Portia and yourself,' Robert answered. 'Didn't I look after you before she met Tristan? Acted as your nanny as well as your housekeeper? Naturally, I came along when her fortunes changed.'

'And why are you still here? Why didn't you leave when she disappeared?' Saskia wanted to know, smelling a rat.

'I was obeying orders,' he said sniffily.

'Whose?'

'Hers.'

'Then where is she?' Caitlin cried suddenly, rising to her knees on the coverlet.

'Don't you believe that Tristan killed her?' Guy asked smoothly, his expression so guarded that Saskia couldn't read it.

'Do *you*?' Caitlin snarled, and Saskia could feel her trembling.

Guy pulled a wry face. 'You know what they say, "Hatred is the other side of love", and there's no doubt that he loved her.

'He told me that his love changed to loathing,' Caitlin said.

Guy gave a savage laugh. 'He couldn't keep up with her. She was like a dark comet blazing across Lyons Court. No one who knew her intimately expected her to be faithful to him, or to any man for that matter. You should ask your friend, Banan Driscol. He didn't only paint her portrait, but fucked her as well. And he wasn't the only one.'

'Including you?'

'Including me. We'd been dabbling in sex together since we were adolescents. Tristan was livid when he found out. We let him know deliberately. It was a great laugh. I've never seen a man so indignant. Comical to watch.'

Caitlin became very still and Saskia watched her as, with calm dignity, she asked Guy, 'Tell me the truth. Did he kill her or did she run away?'

'Ah, that's the sixty-thousand dollar question,' he answered flippantly, and sat beside her and turned her over so that he could admire his palm imprints on her rump. 'Enough talking,' he snapped suddenly.

He nodded to Robert, who handed him a small dark green bottle. Guy unscrewed the cap and drizzled a measure of oil on to the dimple at the base of her spine. Saskia watched it trickling down Caitlin's crack and into her labial groove and wished it was herself whom he caressed. His hands skimmed over Caitlin's skin, gliding into her slit and then out again, spreading a shiny layer of oil over the red marks left by his spanking. She gasped and threshed as he delved between her legs and frigged her little button. Then, before he brought her to completion, he poured more oil on to her backside and rolled a fresh condom up the length of his newly erect penis and oiled that, too.

Saskia guessed what was coming next. He dragged Caitlin down till her legs hung over the side of the bed, then pushed pillows under her hips, raising them, her dark fissure having a polished sheen. Now he stood between her thighs, holding the base of his cock and running a hand over the greasy surface.

'Not again,' Caitlin moaned piteously as he pressed against her tightly closed anus. Saskia was terribly aroused, slipping her hand down to her fork, opening her folds and spreading her copious juice up and over her clitoris. The pleasure was acute.

'It's all right, Caitlin,' she murmured. 'It will be easier this time. Just relax.'

He pressed his cock home, just the first two inches, stretching Caitlin's nether hole and she rolled her head from side to side, struggling to escape yet wooed into acceptance by his hand beneath her, the middle digit palpating her bud. Saskia watched as Guy caught his breath. With her finger rousing her own miniature penis, she could imagine what he was experiencing; the tightness of that dark passage, the dash of cruelty mingled with mastery, the thrill of breaching forbidden territory. She wished, and not for the first time, that she was a man. A strap-on dildo was the closest she could get. Now she wanted to use one on Caitlin.

Guy thrust harder, inserting more of his stiff organ into Caitlin, driven on by her cries. Saskia wondered if such tightness was painful to him, like forcing a ring over a too large finger, but he went at it with ferocious strength, going ever deeper. Now the quality of Caitlin's cries had changed, becoming an ululating wail of desire as he drove on tirelessly, his body bumping against the soft globes of her bottom. He gave one final burst of energy and shuddered. Saskia knew he had exploded into orgasm and felt the liquid fire of her own climax flood through her.

'It shouldn't have happened,' Caitlin said, dashing tears from her eyes with the back of her hand.

'Don't be such a wuss,' Saskia replied, lounging in the passenger seat and showing not the smallest sign of remorse. 'It was a laugh. I enjoyed witnessing your second de-flowering.'

'I don't want to think about it,' Caitlin snapped back. 'Guy's a pervert, a cheat and a liar. I don't know if I can believe a word of what he says about Tristan and Portia.'

Saskia yawned widely. The digital clock on the dashboard showed three-thirty. 'Who gives a toss?'

'I do. I want to know if he's free to marry me, or even if I want him to be.'

'Having doubts?' Saskia said sleepily, and lit up another cigarette.

'I need to talk to him,' Caitlin said, and pulled up outside High Tides.

'Didn't you enjoy any part of tonight?' asked Saskia slyly, and reached over and rested her slim hand on Caitlin's knee. 'I thought you might have found it educational, at the very least. Can I come to bed with you for what's left of the night, now that you've supped on the delights of Lesbos?'

'No,' said Caitlin firmly, steering the car round to the back where the stables, now garages, stood.

'But you enjoyed it?'

'Yes. Another time, another place, perhaps, but just for now I'm trying to sort out my feelings for

Tristan. Goodnight, Saskia.'

Amazing herself by her own firmness, Caitlin took off to her suite to shower away the scent of Guy's sex from her body, and also that of Saskia, then to drop into bed and sleep; cleansed and alone. She had much to think about, not least was her own emotions regarding being sodomised. It had hurt, she had felt humiliated and had wanted to leave Lyons Court as soon as it was over. Now her head ached and her arsehole was sore, but she had never felt more wanton or shameless in the whole of her existence. The big bed beckoned and suddenly she couldn't be bothered to shower, kicking off her shoes, flinging back the duvet and dropping on to the mattress then, with a sigh of sheer exhaustion, hefting the quilt over her and snuggling down in its warm folds. Within seconds, she was asleep.

Late afternoon the next day, she received a telephone call from Tristan telling her to meet him in his favourite place – the rugged half circle of rocks that nursed his private cove. The day was perfect. A light breeze blew little puffs of cloud across an azure sky, with a bright sea running before it.

When she first saw him, nervous sweat dewed her brow. Her nipples rose under her bikini bra, and her clit throbbed confined by the tanga and her Indian-print sarong. She had almost forgotten how handsome he was. So tall and fierce featured. He had a temper, as she had witnessed when she trespassed, and again the chilling thought entered her mind: was he capable of killing?

His arm came round her waist as they strolled and, 'What have you been doing while I've been away?' he asked.

'We've been so busy,' she answered, glad that her eyes were hidden behind sunglasses. It made it easier to dissemble, though what she was about to tell him was fact. 'The warm weather has brought a rash of late bookings. I'm considering extending the building.'

'That busy, eh?'

'It's now the thing to hire suites for business conferences, especially out of season.'

'Clever girl,' he said and his arm tightened about her.

'And how did it go in London? Any news?' she asked, distracted from the main reason for her being there – the need to have her flesh reunited with his.

His face darkened, and he snapped back, 'I don't want to talk about it.'

She did, but maybe this wasn't the moment. He had other things on his mind and she thrilled as she guessed what they were. Glancing down, she could see the extended bough of his cock, swelling behind the fly of his blue jeans. To know that she was desired by this spectacularly handsome man made her breasts ache and her clit quiver.

He took her up the path in the direction of the house, but then diverted along an overgrown track, coming out in a clearing. There, hidden among the trees, was a mock ruined temple – a folly. She'd not seen it before. Up the marble steps, between Grecian pillars and into a small round room where garden chairs were stored, and couches and cushions and pillows for those who wished to rest – or make love.

His impatience was flattering. He couldn't wait to kiss her, his mouth searching hers, giving her divine sensations. Then he undid her bikini bra, and his thumbs rolled over her nipples, arousing her further. Next he found his way under the sarong and into the side of her tang, teasing her more intimate lips and opening the floodgates of pleasure for her. They didn't speak, sinking down on a daybed, hands fumblingly eager to get rid of clothes and concentrate on skin. He peeled off his jeans and his penis leapt out, ready and eager. Caitlin wore so little that it took but a second for her to be naked. Like a famished man at a banquet, Tristan gazed at her most secret region, and she breathed in the warm scent of his sensuality. He caressed the folds of her vagina then found her clitoris, his tongue like slippery satin as she gave herself up to him.

'Oh, yes,' she whispered, her breathing fast and ragged, and cried out her pleasure as she succumbed to a shattering orgasm.

This was his cue; now he sank into her with a long, slow push, his shaft creating deep heat. With her body locked to his, her doubts receded and she could almost believe that they were meant for each other. She clawed at his back, writhing as his movements became frantic. Her legs came up to wrap round his waist, holding him closer and deeper, and she felt him reach his zenith.

Suddenly she felt like a traitor. She had encouraged the attentions of Guy and aided and abetted him in his trespass at Lyons Court. She should tell Tristan, but couldn't bring herself to do so. He obviously knew nothing of the visit of Portia's rascally cousin. Robert must have covered their tracks, and not for the first time. Robert, who Tristan trusted, as he did her. She wanted to confess but couldn't, and unable tell him what was wrong, wrenched herself from his arms. He uncoupled himself from her and she saw the bewilderment on his face that quickly turned from sleepy satiation to dismay.

'What is it, darling?' he asked, fingers in her hair, making her look at him. 'Did I hurt you?'

She moved further away from him, picking up her sarong and wrapping it round herself, wanting to hide her body which had behaved in such a wanton fashion with his enemy. 'No, no,' she said, very low. 'It is nothing you did, just the difficulty of the situation ... the uncertainty of Portia's whereabouts ... the impossibility of our being able to marry.'

'I don't see that it is impossible. All we have to do is wait a few years and then my marriage to her will be declared null and void.' He sat there in all his muscular glory, the type of man she had always wanted and she was having to deny him.

She jumped up, pulling on her top and gathering her belongings. Her mind was quite made up and she dared not linger in case he tried to persuade her otherwise. 'I think we should cool it for a while,' she said, marvelling at the steadiness of her voice. 'Contact me again when you have some solid evidence of Portia's whereabouts. Goodbye, Tristan.'

And she walked away. As in times of terrible stress, she was hardly aware of the journey. To her intense relief, Tristan made no attempt to follow her. She left the woods, crossed the sandy pathway between the dunes and came out in the cove.

The sun was sinking towards the sea, and she made her way to the next bay, the solemn sound of rolling surf in her ears.

CHAPTER

9

'You know, I might as well be the owner,' Belle said complacently, hugging Barry's naked side, feeling their sweat mingling, curling her fingers in his chest hair, one of her legs thrown over both of his. She loved that early hour before the rush began, a time of peace and contemplation and getting in just one more fuck. His cock was morning-hard, raring to go.

'Is she off again?' he enquired drowsily, his palm encompassing one of her breasts. She was big, but so was his hand.

'Yep! Wants to visit the Eden Project with Saskia,' Belle replied, wriggling her hips to indicate that her clitoris needed attention.

'They say it's worth a look,' he said, waking more fully and easing his erection between her thighs. She grabbed his free hand and placed it firmly on her love-bud.

'I know. There's a brochure on the reception desk.'

She was losing concentration, focusing on his blunt glans butting her damp entrance. He moved his pelvis, and it slipped inside. She chuckled. 'He hasn't got his overcoat on. Here, let me,' and she moved away, fished under the pillows, found a condom and fitted it up his length and round his girth.

As Barry dipped his head down between her legs, found her clit and sucked it, Belle's busy mind continued to conjecture on business and Caitlin and her recent hints that, if they expanded, she might like to go into partnership. It was this notion, as much as Barry's skill at cunnilingus, (she'd taught him well), that swept her to the top of the rollercoaster and sent her spinning off into space.

'I thought you'd gone,' Caitlin had said, surprised when, on answering her mobile, she had heard Guy's voice.

'Not quite. I'm hanging around in Newquay. How about you and Saskia coming out for the day tomorrow? They say that the Eden Project and the Lost Gardens of Heligan are stunning. I'm sure Saskia would be up for it. I'll meet you on the quay around ten-thirty. OK?'

'Supposing Tristan sees you?'

'He won't. Robert tells me he's moping about with a face as long as a fiddle.'

'Robert always knows everything,' she had said resentfully. 'He's a snake in the grass.'

'Depends where you're coming from,' he had answered lightly. 'Some people think he's a pearl without price.'

So she had agreed to meet him next morning, and was, in fact, glad of an excuse to get away. Though keeping herself extremely busy and meddling in matters of hotel management that were strictly Belle's province, she had still been unable to stop thinking about Tristan. At times she chided herself for being a fool to turn him away. At others she felt relief, as if she had had a narrow escape.

The quayside was already humming when she strolled down there with Saskia. They both wore shorts, and Caitlin had daringly put on the little pair she had bought at the Lobster Pot. They fitted so tightly that the seam dug into her vertical slit and plumped out the labial wings either side. She would have to be careful if bending from the waist or her female secrets would be on show. Saskia, it seemed, had no such doubts, her fringed denim hot-pants were so skimpy that they left nothing to the imagination. Her top consisted of two triangles upheld by spaghetti straps, her shoulders, long brown legs, bare arms and midriff a caramel hue. She had been taking full advantage of the terrace, the pool, the beach and the sea.

'Gee,' she exclaimed, sashaying along on her high wedge mules, 'how the guys around here stare. You'd think they'd never seen a woman before.'

'Maybe they've never seen one quite so generous with her assets,' Caitlin answered, guiding her to the car park on the quay. 'Have you managed to screw Jon yet?'

'Darling, where do you think I got these teensy things? I mentioned your name, and he was more than willing to oblige. You're right, girl. He *is* hung like a donkey. I'm off down there to have another go. And I simply can't leave until I've had a second helping of Raff.'

'You mean you've already had one?' Caitlin had never got used to the speed with which Saskia moved.

'Of course, petal. What do you think I was doing while you were absorbed in the drama of Tristan and yourself? I got Raff alone in that dinky little flat he occupies. He cooks there, too, you know. Plenty of smeary ice-cream and piquant sauces and all those lovely additions to straight sex. Like me, he appreciates food as much as copulation. He's a master of surprises. I like him.'

They leaned on the stone wall, looking across the harbour. Trawlers bobbed on the water, and stalwart, copper-skinned mariners touted for trade. Their patter was a kind of latter day, 'All aboard the *Skylark*', as they persuaded punters to step aboard smartly painted wherries converted from sail to petrol, for a cruise round the bay.

'There you are, ladies,' said Guy, his arms coming round their waists from behind.

Caitlin turned, very nearly regretting the impulse that had urged her to agree with his proposal. Saskia obviously didn't share her doubts, her smile betokening her excitement and willingness to go along with his suggestions. He was looking delectable, in a loose white linen suit with draped jacket and baggy pants, worn with a vest. His curly flaxen chest hair showed at his throat.

'Is that your car?' she said, as he fired the remote at the black BMW.

'I have use of it,' he replied nonchalantly.

Caitlin sat beside him and Saskia occupied the

back seat. The car had that new, showroom feel and smell. He must be doing well to be able to afford it, she thought, her bottom sinking into the squidgy leather upholstery, the shorts riding high into her crack. She was suddenly possessed of a holiday feeling: no High Tides, no Tristan, no one to worry about. And it was all down to this blond Adonis in the driver's seat, his tapering, aristocratic fingers lightly controlling the steering wheel, as once, not so long ago, they had controlled her.

Queensbury disappeared behind them. They were climbing, coming out on a straight road and heading north. After a while Caitlin saw a signpost, but Guy ignored it. 'Didn't that say St Austell?' she asked.

He slanted her a wicked grin and rested his left hand on her bare knee. 'It did.'

'Then why aren't we going there? Surely that's where both the gardens and the Project are?'

'You're right. I'll bet you're a whiz at mapreading.'

Caitlin felt a stab of unease, even though her thighs were parting of their own volition to permit the caressing of his fingers. 'Where are you taking us, if it's not there?'

'You'll see,' he said calmly, and his middle finger wormed its way past the tight seam of her shorts and stroked the stretched, damp and silky gusset of her minuscule panties.

'But—'

'No buts.' He glanced at Saskia in the driving mirror, adding, 'You've no objection, have you? Let's say we're on a mystery tour, like those coach trips so popular with old biddies. I want you both to hand over your mobiles.'

'Hey, that's tight! It's a part of me,' Saskia grumbled.

'You must do as I say. I'm your master.'

'Where are we going?' Caitlin was decidedly apprehensive.

'Away from this place; Devon as well. We've a long drive ahead, but fear not, I shall take you to a first-class eating house and then we'll carry on.'

'I must let Belle know if I'm going to be late,' Caitlin said, panicking.

'I'll do that for you,' he said, and his voice was so stern and commanding that a frisson of fear and arousal tingled along her nerves and settled in her sex.

'You haven't told us the reason for this elaborate form of kidnapping,' Saskia said sarcastically. 'Really, Guy, for a grown man you are inordinately fond of games.'

'This isn't a game, I assure you,' he snarled, and the severe line of his face made Caitlin's heart pound even more. 'I'm doing you a favour, Caitlin. Taking you to meet someone you've been gagging to see ever since you met Tristan.'

'And who might that be?' she quavered.

'Portia,' he said and accelerated, the car shooting forward like an arrow from a bow.

Portia!

'So she's alive?' she gasped, relief swamping her as it proved Tristan's innocence, yet there was dread and disappointment, too. Now he was still married to the wretched woman!

'Very much so,' Guy replied. 'Why? Did you really believe your beloved Tristan capable of murder? Tut, tut!'

Caitlin sank back in her seat, watching the lights

of the motorway growing more orange as dusk set in. There was no escape. Guy stopped once as promised, but she merely picked at the food though the ancient coaching-inn provided fine cuisine. Once more on the road and he didn't stop again, as his fast car ate up the miles and crossed the borders of several counties. No one spoke and it was dark when they took a side exit, and plunged deep into the countryside. By that time both Caitlin and Saskia were tired, chilled, too, though they had dragged fleeces from their tote-bags, and the feeling of being held prisoner gave Caitlin a sensation that was far from fun.

She was surprised at Saskia's calm acceptance of the situation, but there were so many aspects of her friend's personality that were anathema to her. She probably understood Guy, his motives and inten-tions, having already been there, done that and got the T-shirt.

Trees enclosed them on either side and there were no streetlights. Darkness loomed ahead, and then the headlamps shone on a pair of high wrought-iron gates set in a stone wall that stretched away on either side. There hung a white sign emblazoned with a name: The Old Manse.

The sensor-operated gates swung back, and Guy drove between them. More trees and shrubs and bushes and then a sweeping drive and a large, Gothic-style mansion that admirably suited the drama of their abduction.

'Wow! *The Fall of The House of Usher*,' commented Saskia, getting out and stretching her legs gratefully, then wriggling her shorts down to free the constric-tion around her crotch. 'I hope you've prepared for us, Guy. I could sink a large gin and tonic.'

His lips curled in an ironic smile, and he said, 'I don't think you'll be disappointed by what's on offer.'

He is loving every moment of this, Caitlin thought as he conducted them up four shallow steps and under an impressive arch that spanned the oak front door. She glanced at Saskia, who reached out and gave her hand a squeeze. Then the door suddenly opened, revealing a white-faced, androgynous person dressed in black from head to foot.

'Master,' the creature lisped and stood back so that Guy and his guests might enter.

'Is she waiting, Ash?' Guy demanded, herding Saskia and Caitlin before him.

'She is, master,' Ash replied and before Caitlin realised what was happening, a silk scarf was bound round her eyes. She felt herself being led forward, across parquet to begin with and then the hardness of stone underfoot as she descended, tendrils of clammy air touching her face.

'Saskia. Are you there?' she cried.

'Yes, I'm here.'

'Blindfolded?'

'Of course. It's all part of the plan.'

She's not afraid, so why should I be? Caitlin lectured herself, and she had never felt more thrillingly alive. Denied sight, her other senses were razor-sharp – hearing acute, touch keen, smell accentuated. The staircase wound steeply, then levelled out. Flagstones echoed their footsteps and the smell of joss sticks filled Caitlin's nostrils. Music throbbed in the background. Guy's hand on her arm pulled her to a stop. The scarf was removed.

She blinked in the sudden light, though it was subdued, then stared at the underground chamber in which she now stood. Flame-coloured spots pierced the gloom of the fan-vaulted ceiling. The walls were of an uncompromising harsh grey, hung with racks containing equipment whose purpose Caitlin could only guess. She was disconcerted to find herself encircled by people, all staring at her hungrily. There were men in long, hooded robes open down the front, revealing their cocks – some limp, some semi-erect and others at full stand. Tall men, short men, middle-aged and old, and others, too, boyish and good looking, who wore metal torques with leads attached and leather straps that passed across their naked chests, clipped to belts spanning slim waists. Their PVC trousers were cut in such a way that their testicles were lifted and pushed forward, their arses bare, and their erections on display for all to handle at will.

Some of the women wore evening gowns with transparent skirts that stood out from their hips, showing bare bottoms latticed with the red stripes left by whips. Strident harpies with wild hair and outrageous make-up posed in wasp-waisted corsets and split-crotch panties, their breasts thrusting out boldly, the nipples rouged, pierced or clamped. Can-can dancers in Edwardian stage costumes straight from the Moulin Rouge kicked up their legs, flaunting their nude cracks. Slave-girls stood submissively in the background, arms clasped above their heads, eyes down, making no response as hands, both male and female, fingered their naked sexual parts, tweaked their nipples and dipped into their nether holes.

Champagne corks popped and muscular wait-ers with bare torsos, in bow ties and posing pouches, moved among the crowd with the aplomb of Chippendale artists, bearing trays of drinks or snacks. Wherever Caitlin looked, it was to be confronted by genitalia of all shapes, sizes and both genders. The very air was redolent of sex. What was this place?

Guy, as if reading her mind, whispered in her ear, 'It's a swingers' club for liberated adults, famous among those in the know. The membership fee is astronomic, but we've a long waiting list of those jostling to join our club.'

'Your club? I don't understand.'

'Don't worry your head about it, little one. All shall be revealed,' he said, one hand on her backside, digging a finger under the hem of her shorts. 'Meanwhile, have a drink and lose your inhibitions.'

He snatched two flutes from a waiter's tray, giving one to Caitlin and another to Saskia. It was a lovely, fruity cocktail though it had a slightly bitter aftertaste. She wondered if it contained an aphrodisiac.

The crowd parted like water to let them through, and then they were standing at the foot of a dais and she was staring up at the figure in the flowing black cloak who towered above her. A hood was drawn over the head, hiding the face. Then the person moved and lifted gloved hands and unfastened the emerald clasp at the throat. The robe slithered to the floor and Caitlin was staring at the woman in the portrait – Portia Trevellyan.

Portia kicked the robe aside, her movements as graceful as a prima ballerina's, and she was even more beautiful than her picture. Her flaming red hair coiled in a thick mass of spirals and ringlets round her head and halfway down her back. Her breasts rose from the top of a purple satin basque, and the nipples were red and prominent and pierced, hung with a pair of tiny tinkling silver bells. The corset was long, clinching her waist and ending in a frill that brushed the denuded pubis. The flushed lips of her sex were folded over her clitoris, though the little tip was poking through, a diamond twinkling in its cowl. Purple suspenders trimmed with sequins made a perfect frame for this luscious nudity, attached to the lacy welts of smoky, fine-meshed, seamed stockings, and she wore thigh-high boots, buckled and studded and ending in six-inch heels that made her even taller and more regal.

She strolled down the carpeted steps, and the scent of her body was powerful, the oyster aroma of female juices, the pungency of French perfume. She came to rest in front of Caitlin, and scrutinised her from under heavily mascara lashes.

'So, you are Tristan's new love,' she said in a rich, mellifluous voice. 'Guy has told me about you. We both decided that you needed a little education ... to have your eyes, and everything else, opened to a broader aspect of sex. You won't get this with Tristan, that's for sure. Why do you think I left him?' She nodded to an extremely beautiful youth who trailed behind her, saying, 'Undress her, Todd, and you,' – she pointed to a black man with an impressive physique, dreadlocks and a beaded apron that inadequately covered his cock – 'Get that one prepared,' and she jerked her head at Saskia.

Those who were looking at Portia with bright-eyed expectancy edged a little closer. Others, fully engaged in their own pursuits, occupied alcoves. In one, a lovely woman was tied by the wrists to a cross bar, her toes barely scraping the floor, her legs forced apart by a spreader. She wore the ecstatic expression of a saint undergoing torment as she was flogged by a man in a toga.

In another, a dominatrix in black leather was using a paddle on the bare backside of her partner, a portly man who was wrapped entirely in cling-film, apart from his cock that stuck out through a hole. Even his face was obscured, with small openings to allow him to breathe. His head was bound, too, and he lay on a bench like a swaddled mummy, or a caterpillar's cocoon, only his moans of pleasure betraying any life as his mistress reviled him and walloped him mercilessly.

Further on an elderly person wearing a priest's cassock, was forcing his cock into the fundament of a thin youth who bent over obligingly, while a woman sprawled beneath him, her mouth fastened greedily over his erection. Another female lay between her legs, slurping at the dark, damp fuzz exposed at the long, unzipped seam that ran from her pubis to the arse of her skin-tight, red catsuit.

A nubile young woman and a classically hand-some man occupied a brightly lit shower stall. He was holding her against his body while she faced the tiled wall, and plunging his thick phallus in and out of her rectum. Another man joined them and let go a stream of golden rain that joined the water flowing over the woman's face and body, then he clasped her lover round the waist and proceeded to sodomise him.

Caitlin just had time to take this in before Todd seized her fleece and removed it, followed by her crop-top. She shivered in her white bra and folded her arms over her breasts but Todd would have none of this – he simply pushed them down, unfas-tened the back strap and whisked the bra away.

'No!' she exclaimed as his fingers tugged at the front of her shorts.

'Do it!' Guy shouted and she felt the shocking sting as a short-handled, pliable whip landed across her bare thighs.

Todd completed his task and Caitlin was naked.

'Pretty,' remarked Portia, walking round her and assessing her from every side, then she shot out a hand and gripped Caitlin's mound in her gloved hand. 'Such a fair bush, and only a tiny bit trimmed. Nice breasts, and a minge that cries out to be fucked. Too good for Tristan. He doesn't deserve such a prize. Wouldn't know how to get the best out of it. We do, though, don't we, Guy?'

She let go, and Caitlin's clit was buzzing, stimulated by the harsh, exciting treatment.

'Oh, yes,' he nodded. He had changed from his suit into a robe. A girl slave knelt before him, parted the garment and took his stiff tool in her mouth. 'Not now,' he growled and pushed her away.

His cock was engorged and huge, wet with the girl's saliva. Caitlin's body responded to his male potency and she wanted to lunge towards it, straddle his hips and have that great thing plunge into her.

Saskia was already stripped, apart from her high wedged mules, and joining in the frenzied sexual activity. She lay on the dais with the black man face down between her thighs, working her clit with his big, fleshy tongue while Portia beat them with her tawse, his flesh and Saskia's bearing the marks of the strap that was cut into wicked strips.

Caitlin was frog-marched across the chamber. Her hands were pulled above her head, velvet-lined cuffs snapped round them and then the manacles were chained to a ring dangling from the rafters. Her legs were spread and shackled, and her desire increased by the second, fear overridden by the potent sexual atmosphere. Her bare breasts and crimped nipples, her pussy and arse were fair game for anyone who wanted to use them. She was a prisoner and couldn't escape.

The crowd surged around her and a dozen hands familiarised themselves with her secrets. She felt but could not see the owners of fingers, cocks and tongues that caressed her lower regions, fondled and kissed her limbs and sucked her clit. It was a revelation, something she had never dreamed might happen to her, and she loved it: the focus of so much attention. Wild waves of orgasm started to gather momentum. Someone held her shoulders from behind and a latex-protected cock penetrated her sex. A dark-skinned glamorous woman fingered Caitlin's mound from the front, while she was having her own arse fucked. Everywhere she looked people were enjoying copulation in a variety of ways, and she felt like a deity, selected to be Guy's Chosen One.

He strode up to her and the others retreated, giving way to him. He was the master, and they merely his willing acolytes. He stood facing Caitlin and gripped the underside of her breasts, one sphere in each hand, while his thumbs revolved on the aching tips. Her love-bud spasmed, but she didn't come. She jerked her hips towards him, confessing her need. He tickled her clit but as she gasped and strained after completion, he abandoned it and applied the cane he carried; not in affectation, but as a means of chastisement. She was aware of Portia, watching keenly, of the spectators urging him on, and then she surrendered herself to his will. A curious calm possessed her. She felt herself to be in the eye of the hurricane. She could no longer tell where the pain ended and the pleasure began.

She was untied and about to fall, but Guy caught, lifted and carried her over to a couch with a luxurious plush throw. He laid her on her belly, and poured balm into his palms and anointed her welts, the sting going out of the bruises. She felt his hand beneath her, rubbing the lotion into her furrow, rubbing her clit until she gasped and came in a shower of bliss. Then she felt him lower his body across hers, knees each side of her hips, his cock probing her arse. And she took him without demur, the pain he caused her adding to the convulsions of pleasure shaking her to the core. When he had done, withdrawing and lying to one side, she heard and smelt Portia and was aware of her taking her cousin's place, penetrating her vagina with a strap-on rubber phallus. More pleasure, more wine and a dark exploration of vices she had not thought existed.

'More fun that Tristan, I'll bet,' Portia said triumphantly when, much later, they occupied an ostentatious seigniorial bed in a chamber the size of a ballroom.

'I don't understand,' Caitlin said sleepily, her eyelids so heavy she couldn't keep them open.

Portia cuddled her on one side and Guy on the other. 'You'll hear all about it in the morning,' he said silkily, and Caitlin sank into a great, dark, billowing cloud of oblivion.

'Ouch! I've a bloody awful hangover,' complained Saskia, dragging herself out to the conservatory.

There amidst rare, tropical blooms, breakfast had been arranged on white enamelled garden tables, close to where a small waterfall trickled into an oval, turquoise-tiled pool. 'What the hell was in that cocktail, Guy? It had a kick like a mule!'

The domed roof had been rolled back, and large glass patio doors flung wide, letting in the sunshine. There was a paved terrace beyond, where flowers cascaded from hanging baskets. Terracotta pots were positioned Italian-garden style, with further exotic blooms rioting in tumbling profusion. The atmosphere was one of high-living and plenty, breakfast consisting of sea-food temptingly displayed, muesli with dried raisins, wheaten toast, curls of yellow butter on silver platters, marmalades galore and pyramids of fruit. Whatever Portia and Guy were up to, it was certainly profitable, Saskia concluded.

'It's a potent brew. I acquired the recipe in New Orleans,' Guy replied, his eyes masked by Gucci shades, his body bare save for a bulging jock-strap as he relaxed in a cane chair. 'That's the place where most requirements can be met and every perverted desire catered for, be they for Cajun food, special powders that will stir up the libido and give you the stamina to go on for hours – even spells, if you visit a voodoo practitioner.'

'And you'd know about that, would you?' she said acidly, pouring herself a black coffee and taking a stool beside Caitlin, who looked as if she was feeling even worse than Saskia.

For her own part, except for a thumping head, she had had one hell of a good time. The black man had been only the first of several partners, and, no stranger to orgies, she had entered into the spirit of the thing. Even the soreness of her hindquarters was augmented by thrills as she recalled how she had acquired it. Not only was she able to play the submissive, but she had reversed the role during the course of the evening. She was a first-class dominatrix when occasion demanded. Her fingers itched as she sipped her coffee and observed Guy. She'd like to have him at her mercy. She visualised him under restraint, tied to a bed with silken scarves while she teased and tormented him, whipped and toyed with him, and finally brought him to orgasm; herself, too, seated on his face with his tongue frigging her clit. She had a pretty shrewd notion that he'd appreciate it.

There was no sign of last night's revellers and Saskia assumed they had gone or were still living it up in the dungeons. Portia was sitting on the edge of the pool, wearing a tiny bra and string that exposed most of her gorgeous body. Saskia was aware of her allure, curious to try out this woman who had caused Caitlin so much angst. There was more to her than met the eye. Beautiful voluptuary she might be, but Saskia suspected there was an astute business brain under that Titian hair.

Todd was with Portia, his feet entwined with hers in the rippling pool as he sipped champagne from a cut-glass flute. His torso was bare and he was wearing shorts of such brevity that his cock-tip poked out of the hem banding his left thigh. Portia chuckled wickedly and ran a finger along the reddened slit, making the penis engorge, the narrow space between the material and his skin full to bursting point.

Her eyes switched to Saskia and, 'Come and join us,' she said.

Dripping wet now, Portia's bra became almost transparent, emphasising her luscious breasts and the darkness of her pointed nipples. The G-string outlined her fork, drawn tight into the crease each side, the cleft deeply defined. It was possible to see the bump of her be-jewelled clitoris. Saskia yearned to touch it. She finished her coffee and slipped out of the kimono she'd found. Her own garments had yet to be retrieved from the underground chamber.

The sun was high, beating down on this private paradise, so lush and sensually inviting. It was wonderful to be naked in such a setting, and Portia was the ruler of this realm where Dionysus was worshipped. Saskia waved to Caitlin who rose and walked to where broad steps led into the water. She was wearing a virginal white chiffon gown that clung to her limbs with every movement. Without hesitation, she waded down the steps, the silk billowing out around her. She gave a little shriek, though the pool was warm, and moved towards Saskia, the fabric adhering to her puckered nipples and the wet plumes of her mound.

Portia opened her arms wide and Saskia and Caitlin went into them. They stripped so there was no barrier between her wonderful sex and theirs. Todd tore off his shorts, his stiff prick nudging against all this woman flesh and, within seconds, Guy was with them. They formed a daisy-chain where mouths, penises and cunts were joined in a ring of delight. They swam, gambled and played, every aspect of sexual coupling attempted. Later Saskia lay on the sun-heated terrazzo tiles and took her fill of Portia's fascinating delta, feeling her jerk and hearing her sigh as her clitoris yielded to the experienced coaxing of her tongue.

'Where is Caitlin?' Tristan thundered, striding into the lobby of High Tides.

This dark-visaged, angry man did not intimidate Belle. She'd met his type before, eaten them for breakfast and spat out the pips. 'She was away for the night,' she answered with a cool that did nothing but exacerbate his rage.

'Where?' he roared, making the crystal drops on the chandelier shake.

'I believe she was going to St Austell with her friend Saskia. Not that it's any of your business,' she said tartly.

'Just Saskia?' He stood over her, glowering, and she didn't bat an eyelid.

'No. I overheard a telephone conversation during which she referred to someone called Guy.'

Just for a moment, she thought he was about have an apoplexy. 'Guy? You're sure?' he asked in a strangled voice. 'Did you get a surname?'

'Not then, but someone who called himself Mr Marlow phoned in late last night to say that she and Saskia were taking time out and staying over with him.'

She felt suddenly sorry for Tristan; the big, strong, lordly looking person now seemed utterly stricken. 'Guy Marlow. He's at the bottom of this,' he said slowly. Then he roused into fury, driving his right fist into the left, drawing himself up to his full, impressive height. Belle could now understand what women saw in him.

'I'm sure Caitlin's all right. Saskia will look after her,' she said soothingly.

He was already making for the door, shouting over his shoulder, 'Thank you, Belle.'

***

With his heart thumping and the desire to become the killer people thought he already was, Tristan drove back to Lyons Court and apprehended Robert in the kitchen. He had trusted the manservant, never mind that he had once been Portia's lick-spittle. Once she had gone, he had been glad to have Robert continue to manage the house, never dreaming that he was anything but loyal. On his way back from High Tides he had been recalling a multitude of incidents when Portia was in residence. They had been so close – her and Robert and Guy. Had this continued once she had been reported missing?

Thinking back, he now realised that there had been incidents which should have aroused his suspicions: telephone conversations cut short when he unexpectedly entered a room, Robert had even been secretive about his mobile, and then there had been his mysterious vacations twice a year. He had said that he was visiting his mother in Bournemouth, but the contact number he had left had proved unobtainable.

Robert looked up guiltily as Tristan covered the kitchen floor in a few long strides. 'Has Guy Marlow been here?' he demanded, making the smaller man cringe.

'Mr Marlow? I haven't seen him for years,' he said shakily.

Tristan seized him by the collar, pinned him against the wall and glared into his sweating face. 'You're lying,' he grated. 'Tell me the truth. Did he come here while I was away? Did he meet Caitlin?'

'No! No! Of course not! Why should he?' Robert gabbled, turning a sickly shade of green.

'*You tell me!* And it had better be good or I can't promise to contain myself. If I thought for one moment that he'd laid a hand on her, or involved her in those dirty games he and Portia liked to play . . .'

He set Robert down on his feet with a jar that made the manservant's teeth rattle, then penned him in with his taut arms pressed either side of him, hands flat on the wall. Robert's eyes darted about, desperately seeking an avenue of escape. There was none.

'You've never really liked me,' he whined. 'Not like Guy. I'm one of his favourites.'

Tristan controlled the strong urge to throttle him. 'You're nothing but a dirty pervert, and so is he. Don't beat about the bush. Where is Caitlin? Where has he taken her?'

'Miles away,' Robert said vengefully. 'You'll never find her without my co-operation.'

'Then give it!'

'I'm following instructions, you understand. I'd never, ever betray them, but they've told me to give you their address, but if you tell the police or anyone else, then they'll remove Caitlin and you'll never see her again.'

'Right. Talk. And make it fast,' Tristan said grimly, and within the hour he was on his way to the Old Manse, Portia's house in the depths of Hampshire.

CHAPTER

10

Twirling gently from golden ropes suspended from the ceiling, Caitlin had never known such peace. She was bound in a foetal position and totally relaxed, having abandoned her will to another – no responsibility, not a care in the world. Nothing. It resembled floating or being in the womb. Though strange and disorienting at first, she had followed her master's instructions and allowed herself to be raised and the harness adjusted. Her knees were drawn up to her chest, her hair streamed down and her genital area was fully exposed to those below or on eye-level with her.

By now, she was more at home without clothes, or wearing those outrageously provocative, fantastical garments that revealed much more than they concealed. Two days had passed since her arrival at the Old Manse. At first she had been worried about High Tides, but Guy had permitted her to speak with Belle who had assured her that all was well there, and advised that she enjoyed the break while she could. So, drunk with wine and love-potions and the sybaritic lifestyle adopted by her host and hostess, Caitlin had given full rein to those sensual emotions and yearnings that she had never before fully admitted possessing.

Her carnality took over from reason, and every new sensation tingled through her like fire. She had taken to each experience readily, running the whole gamut of sexual exploration, teetering on the very edge of the unacceptable. Now she was in the dungeon, thrilling to its lurid glowing light, feeling herself to be the sinecure of all eyes – so open, so brazenly displayed. She felt a hand fondling her buttocks, and another fingering her crack. It was wet and slippery and she wriggled her hips and urged the stranger to go further, higher, greasing the bump of her excitable clitoris. She had lost count of the number of times she had erupted into climax.

Someone cranked the pulley and she was lowered slightly. There were hands on her bottom and at her breasts, tugging at the nipple clamps, making her sweat with the pain/pleasure this evoked. A woman stood just out of sight, combing Caitlin's flesh with long, violet-lacquered nails. It wasn't Portia. She was on the divan with Saskia and Todd, while she milked his cock and Saskia tongued her delta, and the young man slipped a hand under Saskia, fingers in rapid motion on her clit.

Caitlin knew that her friend was intoxicated with these mad, bad days, but they must leave this Eden very soon; Saskia to go back to London and Caitlin to concentrate on her hotel. But just for now she was content to stay. Two cocks were swaying in front of her face and she opened her mouth and took the largest inside, then felt the warm dampness of the other pressing into her manacled hand. She was conscious of another male appendage sliding neatly into her vagina, and a finger being thrust into her anal hole. She was completely stuffed, mouth, pussy and arse, and it filled her with divine satisfaction. She gasped and the violet-nailed woman increased the friction on her clit so that she tumbled into the sparkling cataclysm of orgasm.

She caught a blinding flash – someone was taking pictures. She didn't care. Then her carnal partners were thrown aside and a whip struck her with a cruel force that made her stomach clench, her thighs jerk and her sex yield even more of its juice. A hard voice accompanied the blows.

'You're a strumpet, with no shame at all,' Guy ground out. 'What are you?'

'A strumpet,' she gasped, tears oozing from the corners of her eyes.

Another blistering slash knocked the breath out of her. 'What else?' he demanded.

'Master,' she sobbed.

'That's better,' he snapped, administering six more blows in rapid succession. 'I'm your master, and never forget it.'

As if she could! He had dominated her for hours, and this hold he had on her had begun on that very first occasion when he had stalked her, a predator single-minded in his determination to control her.

But meeting with Portia had caused a seismic shift. She was no longer the dreaded rival and enemy, but a voluptuous woman, pleasure bent and willing to share the largesse of her sexual favours. She was nothing like the villainess of Caitlin's imaginings, and Caitlin was more than happy to be here with her.

Guy unfastened her restraints, saying, 'Stand up,' and this command was, like the others he issued, to be obeyed at once. He ran his hands over her trembling body, then pushed her down on her knees, head bowed like a slave. 'Now lie back on the couch and masturbate,' he said.

She was feeling weak and subjugated. Her cleft was wet and her clitoris throbbing. She did as Guy told her. The three persons locked in congress on the divan shifted over to make room for her. She was aware of interested spectators gathering. Guy stood over her, watching. There was a hush, followed by an audible sigh as she ran her fingers round her pussy, dabbled them in her wetness and slathered it over her swollen labial wings and found the source of all bliss – her rampant clit.

'You're beautiful in your need,' whispered Portia, turning from where she had mounted Todd, his prick buried in her denuded slit. 'Go for it, my darling. Let it come.'

Caitlin needed no second bidding. Although she had climaxed many times, this had done nothing but raise her sensitivity and desire. It seemed that the more she had, the more she wanted. She circled her clit, patted and played with it, tantalising it by skirting the tingling head and rubbing each side of the stem. Because she had so recently come, she was able to use delaying tactics, leaving her crack entirely and pinching her nipples, then arching her back and probing herself again, moving against her clutching hand. Release was close, and she was anxious in case Guy orchestrated one of those frustrating scenarios when he stopped her in full flow, teasing her as she was about to explode. Would he do this now?

She rubbed harder, but, 'Take your finger away,' he ordered.

She considered disobeying him. What if she was quick and secretive, didn't thrash around or cry out, but just pressed her clit firmly and brought on the spasms? He'd never know and she'd have achieved a smug little victory and a well-earned orgasm.

Yet though her mind rebelled, her body was obedient to its master. She withdrew her fingers and let her hips go slack.

'I felt your defiance,' Guy said coldly.

'That's impossible,' she returned, looking up at him.

'I know women, and I know you,' he answered patronisingly. 'You love all this, and this, too.'

Giving her no time to breathe, he flipped her over and kneed her legs apart, then plunged his rubber-covered cock between her bottom cheeks and into her arse. He finished her off briskly, frigging her nubbin in rhythm to his own thrusting, and she came with a yelp at the same time that he shot his semen into the condom.

The mobile bleeped, three rings drawing Todd to lift it, then hand it over to Guy. He spoke into it rapidly, his cold eyes glittering, his prick still buried in Caitlin's arse. 'Good,' she heard him say. 'Well done, Robert. We'll expect to see you very soon.'

'What has happened?' Caitlin asked anxiously. She was always nervous when Robert and Guy were in cahoots.

He gave a wicked chuckle, flicked her nipple clamps, and said, 'You'll find out soon enough.

Now, let Todd tidy that mess you made of shaving your bush. I want to see it as pink and bare as Portia's. How about he pierce the labia? It's time you started to wear jewels there.'

The front door was opened at Tristan's peremptory knock. A very tall, very gaunt person stood there; it was impossible to tell its gender. 'I'm Ash,' it said. 'Come in, sir. They are expecting you.'

This surprised Tristan till he remembered that the lines between the Old Manse and Lyons Court would have been red hot after his confrontation with Robert. His heart did a strange little flip in his chest. Soon, if what the treacherous manservant had said was true, he would see Caitlin. And as for Portia? His anger rose to boiling point and he wanted to fasten his hands round her throat and commit that crime of which he had been suspected for so many years. She was a bitch on wheels! And Guy the most despicable of men.

Ash beckoned to him to follow and they went down and down into the very bowels of the house that had once been the home of the parish minister. Now it was God only knew what, but Tristan had a shrewd and uncomfortable idea. When they reached the dungeons, he knew he had been justified in his assumption. He saw the lurid glow, the crosspiece, the whips and flails and all the other accoutrements of weird sexual enjoyment that Portia had wanted when she lived with him.

He registered two things: the first was Caitlin, whose new sluttish, wanton air made her almost unrecognisable. She lolled against velvet cushions on a divan, naked as the day she was born. Even her pubic hair had gone. His second shock was to see Portia lounging beside her, dressed like a priestess of some outlandish cult, feathers, silks, naked limbs, heavily painted eyes, and a gorgeous young man in tow.

Tristan stopped, stared at her, and said, 'Things haven't changed, then, Portia? Still the same cradle-snatching whore.'

Her eyes narrowed dangerously. She pushed Todd aside and rose to her full, impressive height. He noticed that she had put on weight; she was a woman in her prime with a magnificent Junoesque figure. No implants for her. He could vouch for the genuine nature of her breasts.

'And you're the same, too. Still the hypocritical, canting twat who couldn't keep up with me,' she returned nastily.

'I had no interest in so doing,' he growled. 'What you do disgusts me.'

'And what about your little girlfriend?' Portia mocked, cradling Caitlin's breasts and jiggling them at him. 'Does she disgust you, too?'

'Be careful,' he warned, his voice gruff with fury.

'Ask her if she finds all this disgusting, Tristan. Or are you afraid of her answer?' Portia challenged.

'She's submitted to me,' Guy said heavily, appearing at Tristan's shoulder, wearing an ornate damask patterned dressing-gown, opened all the way down the front, his iron-hard erection jutting out. 'I've had her every which way, after I've beaten her, of course. In the mouth, between the breasts, up her cunt and inside her arse.'

Tristan could feel great waves of anger surging through him – blinding rage, the primitive urge to kill, these were the powerful emotions that had possessed him when he and Portia lived together as man and wife. It had been impossible. It was *still* impossible. Looking at her critically, he found that he no longer hungered for the woman and certainly didn't like her. All passion had been spent in that direction, apart from fury.

As for Guy, he had a reputation as a liar. Was he lying now? Glancing at Caitlin's worried face, he read the truth there. She had never been one to keep her cards close to her chest. She was honest. What you saw was what you got, as far as he had been able to ascertain. This was one of the reasons why he loved her.

'Is Guy speaking the truth, Caitlin,' he asked softly, fighting the urge to take her in his arms and hold and comfort her like a frightened child.

She coloured from her breasts to the roots of her hair. Sitting up, she looked him in the eye and said, 'Yes, Tristan.'

It was like an arrow piercing his vitals. 'Why?' he said.

'You were away,' she stammered. 'He came to Lyons Court and told me about your past. I didn't know who or what to believe. He showed me things . . . such things that appealed to a dark side of me. And then we came here and I met Portia and it was all so different to anything I had experienced with you.'

'And it always will be,' Portia interjected pithily. 'Why do you think I left him? He was rich, handsome, and influential, but I needed more.' As she spoke, she waved her followers away, adding, 'There are matters we need to address in private, Tristan.'

'There certainly are,' he agreed tersely. 'You left without a word, taking a number of valuable antiques, to say nothing of money, credit cards, cleaning out of joint bank accounts and cashing in assets. To add to this, you allowed me to be hounded by the police and press. I was looked upon as a psycho, a wife murderer, and am still viewed with suspicion. Why did you do it?'

Portia paced around him, hands on her hips. 'Because I found you insufferably boring.'

His face darkened. 'Didn't you ever love me?'

She gave a careless laugh and flaunted her body. 'I had the hots for you, to start with. Besides, you could provide me with all the material comforts I craved. Guy was in on it, too. He advised me to accept your proposal. He and I have always done everything together. Haven't we, darling?'

'Naturally. We're a team,' Guy said, bent and kissed her full on the lips. She snuggled against him.

'You were nothing but a gold-digger,' Tristan exclaimed. 'A greedy, unprincipled whore.'

'That's not the whole truth,' she teased, raising one leg and using a brisk frottage on her clit. 'At first, I behaved like the lady of the manor, very much so,' she continued. 'But I soon became too bored to keep up the pretence.'

'Whatever I felt for you is in the past,' he said grimly. 'I want a divorce.'

'Do you now? And what do I get in return?' she asked.

'Agree to it, and I'll say nothing about the articles you stole.' He had come prepared to haggle. 'You'll tell the police the whole story and get them off my back. You may need a lawyer for they'll probably prosecute you for wasting their time. Come clean about how you hid your identity, cashed in my money and set yourself up here.'

'I went abroad first,' she said. 'Got the hell out of it for several months, then this property came on the market and it was just the place Guy and I were looking for.'

'Did you need to lie and use such an elaborate deception?'

She gave a mischievous chuckle. 'It was exciting, thrilling and amusing . . . just to stretch the bounderies and see how much I could get away with. But you wouldn't understand anything about that, would you, Tristan?'

'I left youthful recklessness behind me long ago. I found you exciting once.'

'I jerked you out of your complacency, but it didn't last long. You wanted me as a brood mare, someone to help run the local women's groups, organise jumble sales, fêtes and church bazaars. It just wasn't my scene. But I'd have had a stab at it if you had only agreed to let me turn the basement into a fetish parlour and torture chamber, like I've done here. There's money in it, Tristan, besides personal satisfaction.' As Portia spoke, she turned her attention to Caitlin, running a hand lightly over her face and tip-tilted breasts.

'I had no interest in your decadent schemes,' Tristan retorted, recalling every last detail of their endless arguments on the subject. 'I wouldn't let you turn Lyons Court into a brothel.'

Portia threw back her fiery red mane and laughed loudly. 'There you go again! So old-hat. Brothel, indeed. What we have here is an exclusive club.'

'I don't want to discuss it,' he said firmly. 'Will you agree to a divorce?'

She shrugged as if the discussion bored her to pieces. 'All right,' she conceded. 'I want to be free anyway. There's a title in the offing – an elderly duke who is in love with me – all I have to do is beat him with a wet lettuce leaf while he's wearing one of his mama's dresses and he jerks off all over the place. There's still a lot of lead in his pencil, and I fancy being a duchess.'

Tristan looked down at Caitlin and asked, 'Are you ready to go back to Cornwall?'

'Yes,' she said, but it was more because of High Tides than him.

'I'm due back in London,' chipped in Saskia. 'But be sure I'll be visiting, Portia.'

'And you, Caitlin?' Portia asked. 'Will you return to join in the fun here?'

'I don't know,' she answered, gathering up her clothes and starting to put them on.

And Tristan, watching her, wondered if there was any future for them.

'You can't marry him,' Portia insisted, arm in arm with Guy. 'Not a girl like you that has such unplumbed depths of sensuality. You'll be completely stifled by the parochial, humdrum life he leads. Don't do it, girl.'

'I shall be contacting my solicitor at once and start divorce proceedings,' Tristan said.

'Do that, darling, and then leave us alone to party,' she answered patronisingly, and patted his cheek.

If ever Tristan had been filled with the almost uncontrollable urge to strike her, it was then. Once more she had ruined his life; his relationship with Caitlin would never be the same again. He stalked from the house in silence, aware that Caitlin and Saskia were somewhere behind him. He was silent, too, on the journey to Cornwall, dropping them off at High Tides and retreating to his stronghold to think things through and plan his next move.

It was one of those warm, sunny days that an Indian summer drops into the lap of autumn. Almost two months had passed since Tristan had shut up Lyons Court, left it in charge of a caretaker and departed for fresh fields and pastures new.

What he had said exactly was, 'I'm going away for a while, Caitlin. They say travel broadens the mind and it seems that mine is in dire need of a vacation.'

'But where are you going? What about us?' she had asked, when he came to High Tides to say goodbye.

He had been avoiding her since their return from Hampshire, and finally he dropped this bombshell. His attitude was remote that morning, his expression withdrawn. She knew that she had hurt him badly, but what was done couldn't be undone, neither would she have wished it so. There were things between them that would never have been resolved had she not behaved as she had. A lengthy separation would make or break them.

'There can be no "us" yet,' he had said resolutely.

'But in the future?' she had persisted, struggling to hold back the tears.

He had almost cracked then, but kept control and said, 'I'll be away till next summer, spending much of the time in America. We'll meet on my return and take it from there. We may find that one or other of us no longer desires to be anything more than friends. Or, we may be so much in love that we can't live without being together. In any case, I'm going to "seek myself, and loosen up", just as Portia suggested.'

He had left soon after and Caitlin had cried hard, then pulled herself together and with the help of Saskia and Belle, set about changing her appearance as well as her take on life. She had worked hard in the hotel, was now slimmer, her long hair styled and streaked with gold. She used more make-up, cunningly applied, and had an assured manner that endeared her to clients and staff alike.

Bella and she were now partners and anticipating a profitable winter season. Saskia had returned to London and Banan was staying with her during his art exhibition. So, left to her own devices, Caitlin was taking cookery lessons with Raff that went on far into the night and generally ended up with them licking their latest recipes from the secret hillocks and hollows of one another's bodies. He certainly was a master chef.

Today, however, she was having time off and was on her way to the quay to meet Jon. He had promised to take her out in his boat. They had been meeting frequently, but somehow there had never again been the opportunity for intimacy. Now, walking briskly towards the Lobster Pot, she hoped that could be rectified this afternoon. He had promised to take her across to Tristan's island, the bird sanctuary called Bard's Peak. There was no fear of anyone apprehending them now, and the knowledge that she would be doing something he had forbidden made the adventure doubly thrilling.

She was early and slackened her pace. Jon waved to her from his shop and indicated that he'd be right out. She perched on the harbour wall, waiting for him. Queensbury was almost deserted. The holiday-makers had returned to their respective towns and the children were back at school. Only the ubiquitous gulls screamed and swooped, quarrelling with other birds over rotting crabs and particles of waste food. Caitlin studied several boats bobbing at their moorings, recognising the *Ariadne*. Jon had already proudly pointed her out. Now he came across the cobbles and hauled Caitlin to her feet.

He led her round to where his boat was anchored, and, grinning at her hesitancy, held her hand and helped her from the solidity of the stone-built quay to the unsteadiness of the deck. The space was restrictive and Jon a large man. She was very aware of him as her breasts brushed against his arm, and she was vividly reminded of that moment in the changing cubicle when he had taken her without preamble.

Oh, she missed Tristan, but she had been awakened to pleasure's bounty, visiting the Old Manse on several occasions since his departure. Todd had shaved her pussy, but it was Guy who had pierced her outer labia and inserted gold keepers on which he sometimes hung thin chains bearing little weights, just to remind her that he was her master. Her navel, too, had been pierced and ornamented with a diamond stud. She liked to show this off, wearing low-slung hipsters.

She knew she had changed, and wondered if Tristan would find her too different when he returned. Her own attitude towards sex had altered; she now recognised that one could have the most fulfilling of encounters with male or female partners, and that terrible emotional state called love didn't need to come into the equation.

Now she glanced around the *Ariadne*, expecting to be aboard a weather-beaten fishing boat but, instead, finding herself on the deck of a well painted cruiser, with brass and chromium fittings, a glassed-in cabin for the helmsman, and a further door leading to lower quarters.

'Go below and take a look around,' Jon invited.

She did so and was amazed at the compactness of the living area: a saloon, a galley, a shower unit and lavatory, and a cabin with a double bed. It was furnished in a strictly masculine style. Caitlin couldn't wait to get him down there, undo the strings of his jogging pants and give him the best blow job he'd ever had. She was aware of the throb of the engine and movement as he steered the *Ariadne* out of the harbour to the open sea. The waves were choppy and she staggered up the companion way and went to stand beside him in the shelter of the wheelhouse.

He gave her a crooked smile, but kept his eyes on the water where, in the distance, the dark bulk of Bard's Peak loomed ever larger. 'I've brought a picnic,' he said. 'The "twitchers" won't be about. It's getting too late in the season.'

'Who are they?' she asked, having difficulty in restraining her impulse to rub her palm over the pronounced bulge distending the loose front of his joggers.

'Bird watchers,' he answered. 'They have permission to set up hides on the island and observe. No one else, except the bailiff, is permitted to set foot there.'

'A picnic in Tristan's forbidden territory,' she answered, smiling at the idea.

'He has too much, that man,' Jon commented as the island blocked out the skyline and he steered the boat alongside a jetty, then dropped anchor and threw a rope across, the loop coiling round a stanchion. 'But he doesn't have you, Caitlin, not at this moment in time. I do.'

He was carrying a blanket and a picnic basket but they barely made the shelter of a cove at the base of the cliff. Before she realised what was happening, he had flung down the rug, seized her in his arms and kissed her hungrily on the lips. He tasted of the sea spray dewing his beard. Her knees turned to jelly and she clung to him. He removed his mouth, smiled into her face, then laid her down and sprawled beside her – sturdy limbs, strong arms, big hands, a genial hunk of a man.

He threw a leg over hers, parting them, his knee pressed between, then undid her fleece and reached under the hem of her T-shirt, pushing it high till her breasts were exposed in an under-wired bra. He cupped one breast and lifted it from its lacy basket, rubbing his broad thumb over the puckering nipple. Caitlin gasped, and the seam of her tight jeans cut into her crotch as she gripped his leg and masturbated herself against it. Jon immediately sprung the button at her waistband and unzipped her fly. In a second, her jeans were down round her knees, her panties following suit and her bare and jewelled cleft was bare to his gaze.

He stared at it in amazement, and she was smugly pleased to have surprised this almost unshakeable person. 'When did you have that done?' he asked, rotating the gold labial rings.

'Not long ago,' she answered calmly, though her clit was vibrating with the movement of the keepers.

'Where?' He took her hand and placed it on the

ties of his jogging pants. She needed no further instruction, but undid them, drawing out his huge, erect cock.

'I've friends who have taught me about many things,' she answered softly, playing with his fiery pubic bush and caressing that mighty member.

'I'd like to meet them,' he said, and, lowering his head, burrowed into her cleft and dived the tip of his tongue into one of the rings. At the same time, he started to massage the head of her clit, rousing within her such sharply blissful sensations that she came on a surge of passion that shocked her from head to foot. He lifted his head to look at her, smiling to see her expression of complete and utter satisfaction. His fingers did not leave her, smoothing in the liquid that flowed from her vulva, spreading it over her labia, her still swollen clit, and each side of its stem.

Caitlin lay still, enjoying the warmth of the day, the heat of his body, the feelings his fingers were producing within her. At first, she didn't think she could come again so soon, but it was like a continuation – gathering like wavelets on the shore, getting larger, more insistent until she was panting, begging Jon not to stop, legs wide, pelvis arched, shameless in her frantic desire for another orgasm. He did not disappoint her.

It still wasn't enough. He rested, drew her head against his shoulder, the brushed cotton of his tartan padded shirt smooth under her cheek. She liked this feeling of security, but her rampant clit demanded more sensation. She reached down and opened herself with her hands and he slid his fingers inside her, copying the movements of intercourse. He thrust in and out and his thumb rotated on her clit.

She moved into him, clinging with her arms, so hot that the sweat was pooling at her collar bone and trickling down her spine. He released the orgasmic tension for her and she cried out.

But now she wanted something larger, thicker and longer than mere fingers, and tugged at his clothing, needing flesh on flesh, a throbbing male prick jarring her cervix and massaging her inner walls. He kicked off his loafers, removed his trousers, rolled on a condom and tugged her denims down the rest of the way. Then, without more ado, he was on her and in her, and she was straining upwards so that her pubic bone grazed his cock-root. He pumped and thrust and, looking into his face, she saw that it was screwed up as he approached his ecstasy. Then she felt his deeply embedded prick twitching as he poured his libation into her.

As always with the man she had just fucked, Caitlin was awash with an almost maternal tenderness for him. She held him close, and gazed past his broad shoulder, seeing the dark green of the towering rocks, the slash of azure sky glimpsed between them and listened to the rush and hiss of breakers and the calls of the birds who did not desert Cornwall, but stayed there all year round, come wind, shine and high water. And so would she, making it her home, running High Tides, mistress of all she surveyed and, maybe – but only maybe – in the fullness of time, marrying Tristan and becoming the lady of Lyons Court, too.